EVERLASTING MAGIC

The Thorne Witches Book 12

T.M. CROMER

CHAPTER 1

$\mathcal{E}$velyn Thorne popped a piece of expensive chocolate into her mouth and waved a hand to add the final pink and red touches to the white, five-foot tree she displayed in her living room year-round. It was the one frivolous decoration she allowed herself. Each month she swapped out the ornaments for whatever national holiday was in vogue at the moment. The cheerful little tree always made her happy.

Since it was February, she had her pick of President's Day or St. Valentine's Day. The latter, of course, seemed like the cheerier of the two. Although, it could be hotly debated at this point in her life. Evelyn didn't have a sweetheart to spend the holiday with. No one to buy her chocolates or wine or extravagant jewelry. Oh, she did have her single gal pals, and they'd all adopted the new tradition of *Galentine's* Day. But still, there were times she was a little down in the dumps about her lackluster love life.

She released a heartfelt sigh. All of her family seemed to be paired up with their forever mate. But not her. Never her. Sadly, she couldn't remember the last time she'd gotten laid.

Determined not to feel sorry for herself, Evelyn retrieved the file containing her latest project. Having recently retired from the FBI, she found herself at loose ends. Periodically, she'd consult on unsolved cases for her old boss, Simon Blane. Tall, fit, and intelligent, he was the type of guy she could easily fall for—if he wasn't still mourning his wife of twenty years.

Needing a drink to take the edge off her restlessness, Evelyn snapped her fingers. A flavorful merlot appeared on the coffee table beside a plate of chocolate bonbons. She picked up her wine, smiled, and took a long sip.

Goddess, it was good to be a witch most days.

The ringing of her cellphone cut through the silence, and catching a glimpse of the caller ID, she had to laugh at the timing. Think of the devil!

"Hello, Simon." She grinned as she took another sip of her drink.

"Evelyn." His voice was as rich as the wine in her mouth, and she savored the flavor of both. A shudder of pleasure washed over her, as it did every time he said her name that way—as if no one else in the world existed and she was his main focus.

"To what do I owe the pleasure of your call?" She had an idea, and she flipped open the file in her lap to start reading.

"Have you had a chance to review what I sent over?"

"Doing it now."

"Really? The courier should've dropped it hours ago." He sounded surprised.

Irritation bubbled up inside her. More often than not, everyone assumed she was all work, work, work because she didn't have a relationship to devote her time to.

"He didn't say it was urgent," she said with an annoyed sigh. "Perhaps you should've mentioned it before now."

"Did I interrupt something?" His voice had cooled, turned more formal, and Evelyn wondered if it was in reaction to her waspishness or whether there was something deeper at play.

She debated lying, but what was the point? They were both too old for games. "No. Nothing important, anyway. I was just decorating for the holiday."

"But Christmas is over, and you're a witch." The surprise in his voice made her laugh.

"What's your point?"

"I… nothing… I just hadn't expected you to celebrate a Christian holiday, I suppose."

"Although my gran was a witch, she also practiced the Christian religion until the day she died. Probably to hide what she was in the public eye." Evelyn sipped her drink. "But that's neither here nor there. I was decorating for Galentine's Day."

The creak of leather came through the line, and Evelyn could totally envision Simon leaning back in his chair. He'd be loosening his silk tie right about now and preparing to take a sip of his scotch. An unruly lock of his sandy-blond hair would've fallen forward and rested across his brow. Although Simon always seemed fatigued lately, his skin would still hold a healthy tan, and not a single shadow would be underneath those intense electric-blue eyes. At least, that was how she saw him in her mind's eye.

"I'm surprised you followed in her footsteps. Most witches are pagan if they celebrate at all."

Evelyn settled back into the pillows of her couch and pondered his comment. "Gran always made each of the holidays fun for all of our family. My cousin Mackenzie wasn't into it as much as the rest of us, but I guess that comes with being a psychic. You already know what you're getting for a present."

Simon chuckled, and Evelyn felt the warmth to the marrow of her bones. "I'm guessing you didn't wait until Christmas morning to find out, though. Tell the truth, you either had Mackenzie tell you what you were getting, or you steamed open the packages, didn't you?"

A startled laugh escaped her. She shouldn't be surprised; he was highly observant on his worst day. "I'm not telling. Anyway, Christmas was almost two months ago, and the new year is upon us. Cupid is waking from his nap and likely sharpening the tips of his arrows as we speak."

Again, Simon chuckled. "Be careful. He's a little asshole. You could find yourself in love with a complete stranger. Likely someone you put behind bars at some point."

Evelyn snorted. "Yeah, not a chance. Cupid can fuck himself with his arrow."

"That's the Evelyn I know and adore." Simon's smooth, amused voice created an ache inside her, and she wished he truly *did* adore her.

"Quit buttering me up, Simon Says, and get to the point of your call." His nickname had been a running joke between them for the twenty-two years they'd worked together. Whenever he gave an order, she'd not comply until he would dutifully mutter the words "Simon Says."

"I should've fired you the first time you started that ridiculous game," he said, disgust heavy in his voice.

Evelyn laughed. "Probably. But you love me anyway."

There was a long pause on his side. Finally, he cleared his throat, and in what sounded like a falsely cheerful tone, he said, "What's not to love?"

With a frown and a shit-ton of butterflies in her belly, Evelyn changed the subject back to the file's contents. "Tell me why this case is so important you had to drag me in. For sure, good ol' Petey can't be happy about it."

Pete Wilson was Simon's direct boss, and on more than one occasion, he'd not so nicely directed Simon to remove her from his team. Simon had always refused. Evelyn was positive he'd killed any chance he had of moving up in the ranks because he always went to bat for her.

The chuckle Simon released was genuine, and Evelyn relaxed again. The momentary awkwardness between them was gone.

Note to self, don't mention the word love to him again.

"This involves good ol' Petey."

"What?" She flipped a few pages until she got to the meaty part of the evidence. "Well, I'll be damned."

"Keep reading."

"Why do you sound grim? I hate it when you're grim," she said, with no little trepidation.

"I've been linked to good ol' Petey's nefarious activities."

"Well, fuck!" Evelyn flipped the phone to speaker and dropped it on the arm of the sofa. She took another long drink of wine, then got serious about reading.

"You going to say something?" Simon asked. "Call me horrible names or ask me if it's true?"

"Get real, Simon Says. I've known you half my life. You're innocent."

A gusty sigh came through the line like he'd been holding his breath. "Thank you, Evelyn."

"I'll call you back in thirty minutes after I've waded through what you've sent." She paused before disconnecting. "Simon?"

"Yeah?"

"They've placed you on suspension, haven't they?"

"I would've thought that goes without saying."

"Do you want to do this by the book or the old-fashioned Thorne way?"

She could almost feel his smile through the phone. "I'll leave that up to you. But I know you won't let me down, Evelyn Thorne."

No, she never would.

CHAPTER 2

After disconnecting the phone, Simon tossed it on an end table and crossed to the glass wall to stare out over the city lights. He was tired of Washington, D.C. and the bureaucratic bullshit. What he really wanted was to live in some remote location with Evelyn Thorne and spend the rest of his days making love to her. They'd only leave their bed to eat and shower.

Simon grinned at the fantasy, then shoved it away.

As he turned from the window, his gaze caught on the picture of his deceased wife reflected there. He sobered and walked to the framed photograph. Tiffany, in all her girl-next-door glory, had been his childhood sweetheart. They'd shared all their firsts: dates, kisses, dreams, lovemaking. Three years ago, she developed an aggressive brain tumor, and no amount of medicine or magic could eradicate the disease that had ravaged her mind. In her more lucid moments, she had begged Simon to end her suffering. Those were the days that gutted him the worst. Perhaps a less selfish person would've done as she requested and helped her take her life. But he'd wanted to spend every available moment with her for as long as he could.

"You should pursue Evelyn when I'm gone," Tiff had told him during one of their last conversations. Her standard pain-filled eyes had been fierce. She'd been determined Simon shouldn't go through life alone after she was gone.

"I don't think of Evelyn that way," he'd remind her. "You're my wife, and I love you."

Her face had softened with acceptance, and tears had filled her eyes. "I know, but I don't want you to be sad, Si. You'll shut down and be a shell."

"I have my job and Casper. I'll survive, sweetheart."

"Casper's old, darling. He's liable to go before me."

And he had. Simon's beloved lab died exactly one week and two hours before Tiffany. If it hadn't been for Evelyn's constant diligence and nagging, he'd probably have found a way to join his wife and dog in the afterlife.

But she hadn't left him alone. She'd shown up at his home and moved into the guest room. Evelyn had allowed him precisely three days to wallow in complete misery, then she'd forced him to get out of bed and to shower off the rank unwashed-body smell. Morning and night, she had conjured or prepared a meal and placed it in front of him. And when he barely picked at his food, she threatened to cast a spell to make him consume his required daily calories.

It had been Evelyn who had arranged the funeral services and who had included a mini memorial for Casper. Simon had almost laughed when she'd sprung that one on him. Tiffany would've loved it. Hell, Tiff had adored everything about Evelyn. Could never say enough wonderful things and even tried her hand at matchmaking in the last days of her life.

Simon had lost his temper exactly once.

"Christ, Tiff! Stop already. I don't feel anything for Evelyn other than admiration for a co-worker. I'm not attracted to her that way. Let this asinine idea go!"

Much to his embarrassment, he hadn't known Evelyn was within earshot. Her squeaked "Oh!" made Simon feel like the worst kind of asshole. And other than the first few minutes, she'd somehow buried any awkwardness remaining from the conversation and treated him like she always had prior to his blunder.

But something had shifted inside him after he woke from his seemingly endless mourning. One day, roughly eighteen months after he'd buried his wife, Simon looked at Evelyn. Really looked at her. He saw a woman he not only admired but one he loved. It started as a stray fantasy here or there. One he'd attributed to loneliness. The subtle strawberry scent that drifted to him whenever she would impatiently shove her shimmering hair behind her ears, the way she'd catch the corner of her bottom lip between her straight white teeth whenever she was concentrating, and the sound of her throaty laugh when someone amused her, all worked together to ensnare him in her spell. He had a weakness for intelligent, leggy blondes with soulful blue eyes.

Simon experienced profound guilt every time he looked at her, though, and on the day Evelyn retired from the FBI, he breathed a sigh of relief. Yes, he missed the fuck out of her—she'd been his greatest asset and had become his best friend—but her absence was for the best because he was determined to never again go through what he had with Tiffany. Those endless years of watching someone he loved beyond reason slowly wither away, to be helpless to save her, were pure torment.

No. He'd rather spend the rest of his life alone than experience that a second time.

His phone rang just as he was sitting down to eat.

"Hey, Simon Says." Evelyn's sultry voice washed over him like a tsunami. He didn't try to suppress the shiver of appreciation it caused but instead basked in it.

"Well? What's the verdict?" He set down his fork and picked up his scotch. "Don't hold back."

"As if I ever do," she said with a light laugh. But her next words were more somber. "What they have is damning, Simon. Extremely damning."

"That's what I thought, too."

"Why didn't you tell me you were suspended before now? And how the hell did you get ahold of this file?"

He sighed. "Why, because I didn't want to drag you into this if there was any other option. And how... let's just say I still have friends in high places."

"Okay, but to answer your earlier question, this doesn't have a by-the-book solution. I think we're going to have to go the badass Thorne route."

Despite the severity of her observations, Simon smiled. He liked her forthright attitude, and pretty much everything about Evelyn made him smile. "So what's our next step, O wise one?"

"Well, I'd say a meeting for you to brief me on all things Pete Wilson related. I'm sure you know stuff about him that isn't in this file. We can set up a plan of attack from there."

"When?"

"Are you dressed?"

Because her comment came on the heels of his lurid fantasies, he choked on a sip of his drink. Fire burned his throat, and he blinked the tears away as he coughed up a lung.

"Sorry, Simon." She didn't sound sorry; she sounded highly amused.

"Unless you intend to go there, you shouldn't joke about such things, little girl. One day it will be your undoing."

Her sharp inhale was unmistakable, and Simon smiled. That would teach her to tease him.

"Well, if you're fully clothed, I can pop over now."

The devil on his shoulder prodded him with his pitchfork. "And if I'm not? Do you still want to pop over?"

The long pause on the other end of the line worried him. Perhaps he'd gone too far and come off as more of a pervert or a creeper. He was unpracticed with flirting.

"I'll be there in ten minutes," Evelyn said in an odd voice.

It left him to wonder whether she preferred him nude or fully clothed.

CHAPTER 3

Immediately before her scheduled teleport, Evelyn scried to see the layout of Simon's living room. It would've totally sucked had he moved the couch to a previously empty area where she'd elected to pop in. She had enough cushioning on her ass without having a real one embedded there.

The mirror showed Simon sipping a beverage with a longing look on his face. She could only assume he'd been thinking about Tiffany. The sadness of it all tried to overwhelm Evelyn, but with the brisk efficiency she was known for, she shoved it away.

Yes, she cared for Simon. But she wouldn't pine for him. Life was too short, as Tiff's death had proven. If Simon couldn't or wouldn't love her, then Evelyn was going to be okay. Perhaps not ecstatically happy, but content. She'd never lacked for lovers in the past, and she wouldn't in the future if it came to that. As a witch, her aging had slowed to a sloth's pace. At forty-four, she still had the body of a thirty-five-year-old woman, and her body would remain looking that young for another thirty or forty years minimum. Attracting the opposite sex was never a problem. And if the part of her heart belonging only to Simon awoke now and again to annoy her, well, she'd find a way to gently put it to bed again.

Inhaling a centering breath, she closed her eyes and drew on her magic. As her cells warmed, she visualized where she intended to go. Except when she finally did arrive, it was to land directly on top of Simon! Seemed her heart found a way to override her calm, collected mind.

Dammit!

"Well, this is a surprise," he murmured as his free arm wrapped around her waist. Was his hand riding low on her hip? It *felt* shockingly low, as if his next move would be to grip her ass.

"Hi. Just thought I'd drop in," she quipped, praying to the gods he didn't hear her thundering heart as loudly as she could.

He grinned, and Evelyn couldn't help an answering smile.

"You're usually a little more elegant in your landings." His gaze grew contemplative and dropped to her lips, where it lingered for a lifetime. Ever so slowly, he shifted his attention upward, taking in every inch of her looming face until he locked eyes with her. "Out of practice, or were you flustered by the idea of seeing me naked?"

A tell-tale flush washed up her neck and over her cheeks. Her face heated considerably as she felt his body's reaction to her nearness.

"Do you want honesty, Simon Says?" Her question came out husky and sounded nothing like her standard cool tones.

"Always."

"Then yes, the idea of you naked is hot as fuck."

His dick grew harder and pressed insistently against her abdomen. It was his turn to blush. She had to admit, the color tingeing his cheekbones looked deliciously good on him.

"Are we going there, Evelyn?" he asked softly.

She was in for heartbreak if she pursued this. He still loved Tiffany, and any sexual relationship with *her* would be to scratch an itch. But she'd be damned if she could climb off him.

For a second, his hand tightened, and his pelvis tilted to press his sex against hers. Then he sighed and dropped his arms to his sides, miraculously keeping the contents of his glass intact.

Evelyn sat up and would've moved away from him if he hadn't

gripped her knee. Stuck straddling him, she raised her brows in question.

"I need to remember this." His tone was rough with something that resembled desire.

Taking a chance, she said, "For your spank bank later?"

Simon barked a laugh, surprising one from her.

In slow increments, the humor left his face. With the thumb on his right hand, he traced small circles up her thigh, shifting ever closer to her center. He stared up at her as if she held the key to his happiness.

Perhaps she did if he wanted to stay out of prison.

Reality came crashing back.

"This is a dangerous game, Simon," she whispered past the sudden lump in her throat. When he didn't immediately stop, she gripped his wrist. "There's no coming back from a one-night stand. Not if we wish to remain friends."

"One night?" With his eyes squeezed tightly shut, he thunked his head back on the carpet. "Right."

His erection hadn't gone down, and Evelyn could feel his thick length between her parted thighs. Warmth grew where their bodies touched, and all she could think about was how hot he was. Or maybe it was from her. At this point, she didn't know which of them was putting off such scorching heat. At any moment, she could remove their clothing with a simple finger snap. In another, they could be joined in the ages-old mating dance.

Goddess, how she wanted that.

Wanted him.

She hadn't realized he'd lifted his lids and was staring up into her troubled face until he asked, "Would it be so terrible, Evelyn?"

"For us to hit it and quit it?" She nodded and looked away. "I can't, Simon."

"Understood. But could you please stop rocking your hips like that? I haven't cum in my jeans since I was in my teens."

She froze in horror. *Jesus!* She'd been mindlessly dry humping him!

"Hey." He cupped her neck and gently pulled her back down to rest on his chest. "It's okay, babe. Really."

"Crikey, Simon," she croaked into the crease of his neck. "I was fucking you with our clothes on."

He snorted a laugh. "My only complaint is the clothing."

She giggled and dropped a kiss against the rough skin of his throat. "That's why I love you."

For the second time in as many minutes, she went motionless.

What the fuck, Evelyn?

"Uh, I mean..." Yeah, she had nothing. No ready excuse to make this awkwardness better.

"I know. I love you, too."

Positive he didn't intend it the way she did, she decided to cut her losses and change the subject. "So, do you want to lie on the hard floor to discuss this case, or should we move this to the couch?"

"Don't say the word hard. I'm trying to get Junior to go down. For that matter, don't say couch or anything that might be construed as an invitation until my body gets the memo you and I aren't happening."

She couldn't stop her bubble of laughter.

"Not helping, woman. Your breasts are brushing against me with every giggle."

"Poor Simon Says," she cooed.

He lifted his head and sent her a hopeful look. "Wait! Are we back to that game? Because Simon can very easily say you must kiss him."

"Hmm." Giving in to temptation, she brushed her fingertips along the softness of his lower lip. "I like the way your brain works."

"It's not my brain doing the thinking here, Evelyn. In fact, it's my dick that's trying to take charge."

CHAPTER 4

Simon silently lamented the loss of Evelyn's curvaceous body when she rolled to her feet. Goddess, he'd felt like he was in a never-ending wet dream from the second she arrived and landed on him. He was positive she hadn't meant to knock him flat or to do any of the wonderful things her body had done while she'd been covering him. More's the pity.

It hadn't occurred to him he hadn't moved until she reached a hand out to him. Allowing her to help him up, Simon stood but didn't release her hand.

"Are we good?" he asked softly. "I don't want a weirdness between us. Your friendship matters too much to me."

She averted her gaze and smiled tightly. "Of course."

When she would've pulled away, he tugged her hand and drew her back around. "What did I say wrong?"

"Nothing."

He knew her well enough to know she was lying. "Evelyn. Look at me."

She closed her eyes instead.

Had he not been watching her closely, he'd have missed the compressed lips and the hard swallow. He felt like a fucking prick for causing her distress. "Tiffany always said I had the sensitivity of a jackass. And she was likely right because I don't understand what I've done to upset you. Please tell me."

With a shake of her head, she opened her eyes. The sadness she displayed pierced his heart.

"What is it?" he asked hoarsely. "Tell me so I can fix it."

"You can't, Simon. You just can't."

"Don't I get to know what the problem is?"

"Not if you want to leave me with even a shred of dignity," she replied with a brittle little laugh.

And just like that, the lightbulb went off, and he understood. "You're in love with me," he said with wonder. "Not just friendship."

Her eyes turned cool, and her full mouth thinned as it turned down.

His own stupid soul took flight, doing loop-the-loops and shouting "Hell, yeah!" all the while.

"I'm in love with you, too, Evelyn," he confessed.

She inhaled sharply, and her vulnerable look almost did him in.

"I don't know when it happened," he said in a low voice. "But one day, I realized you've come to mean everything to me."

"Oh, Simon."

He spread his arms, and she dove into them, winding her arms so tightly around his neck, he thought he'd strangle.

His fear was a live thing, and he hated the weakness inside him that let him confess to these life-changing emotions. Because for sure, he didn't know how to move forward from here. He didn't want to take the chance on another relationship doomed to tragedy, but he also couldn't let Evelyn believe he didn't care.

She drew back and cupped his face with her palms, and in slow increments, her beautiful wonderment at his admission turned to bemusement. Dropping her hands, she backed away.

He did nothing to stop her.

"But you don't *want* to love me," she stated flatly.

"No. I don't."

Her lips rounded in an O, and she covered her mouth with her hands.

All his joy from a mere minute ago morphed into dread. How could he tell her he feared committing to another relationship? His mother had died when he was only five. His father, a shell of his former self, followed less than a year later. And just when he'd started to care about the elderly aunt who had taken him in, she was shot in a drugstore robbery. His brother, Trevor, two years his senior, had disappeared the day Simon turned sixteen and left him to his own devices. Was it any wonder he'd latched on to Tiffany with everything he'd had?

But she died, too.

"Loving you is a curse, Evelyn," he said gruffly.

"What the *fuck*, Simon?"

Her indignation made him rethink how he'd phrased it, and he winced. Rubbing the spot between his brows, he tried to explain. "Not you. Not *your* love. But my loving you. My love is a curse to anyone unfortunate enough to be the recipient."

Knowing he was screwing it up royally, he stopped speaking and held his breath, hoping beyond hope she understood and didn't expect him to bare his entire tattered soul. He wasn't sure he could.

Finally, she nodded, albeit slowly as if whatever she was trying to process was righting itself in her brain. "You think *you're* the one cursed?"

"Yes."

A corner of her mouth curled up, and she shook her head. "You're wrong. But you'll need to be the one to come to terms with it."

"I'm not. Wrong, that is." He started to run a hand through his hair and was startled to find his forgotten drink. The need to consume the alcohol was stronger than anything else, so he chugged it down past his tight throat.

"Your thinking is flawed, Simon Says."

Her matter-of-fact attitude irked him.

"How do you figure?"

His snappishness caused her to lift her brows and narrow her eyes in warning. He almost smiled. Evelyn didn't take shit from anyone, and most especially not from him.

"Pour me a glass of wine, and I'll tell you."

She sauntered over to the sofa, and Simon couldn't tear his gaze away from the play of her shapely hips as they swayed from side to side. Abruptly, she stopped and twisted her upper body just enough to challenge him. "Like what you see?"

Busted.

He couldn't prevent the grin at her sassiness. "Abso-fucking-lutely."

Less than three minutes later, he was back with a glass of her favorite merlot and another two-finger shot of scotch for himself. "So tell me, wise one, why is my thinking flawed?"

"Life is messy, and people die, Simon. It's a fact. Tiffany—" Evelyn paused and blinked away the forming tears "—Tiffany's illness was tragic, and we both loved her. But by your measuring stick, I should never let another person become my friend because they might contract cancer and die."

Although he'd come to grips with his wife's death, this conversation still made him raw and edgy. Tiffany, when alive, was flawed and needy at times. He'd never admit aloud that he'd sometimes felt overwhelmed by her demanding nature, but he had loved her, and in the end, she was selfless in trying to see to his future happiness. So discussing her now, even with another person who had loved and respected her, pissed him off.

"I know that," he snapped. "And leave Tiff out of your conjecture."

"Of course. Why don't we change the subject to the reason I came by?" Evelyn's lovely face lost all expression, and she pasted on a composed mask of politeness.

Simon fucking hated when she did that. It was as if all the fun in her dried up, and she became all manners and cold, calculating stranger. Too many times in the past, she'd thrown up the barriers to her true self, and it made him want to rip those goddamned walls right down.

"I don't like being handled, Evelyn," he growled.

One perfectly groomed brow shot up. "Is that what I'm doing?"

"You damned well know what you're doing. Knock it off."

"Perhaps I should return when you're in a better frame of mind," she suggested coolly.

"I'm never going to be in a better frame of mind. My wife is dead, I am being set up to look like a dirty agent, and I've had an erection for the entire time you've been here."

They both stared at each other, him in horrified wonder, after he uttered that last unnecessary bit. *What the hell made him say that?*

The spark of humor returned to Evelyn's face, and Simon had to give her credit for not dropping her gaze to the evidence of his arousal.

"Right. Pete Wilson," she said.

"That was enough to kill any desire I have," Simon muttered before taking a hearty sip of his drink.

She sputtered a laugh. "I thought it might."

CHAPTER 5

For the next forty-three minutes, they discussed all of Pete's nefarious activities and ties to the criminal world. The list of the Bureau's grievances against the man was a mile long. Somehow, the bastard had found a way to plant evidence against Simon over the years, as if he was setting him up to be the fall guy. Evelyn said as much.

"I know," Simon replied.

He was sprawled out on the opposite sofa, arm over his face and powder-blue shirt untucked with the buttons undone.

Casual elegance in male form.

She wanted to eat him up.

But she wouldn't.

Despite Simon's confession of love, he was still hung up on his deceased wife. That was something Evelyn couldn't—and wouldn't—fight. She almost wished he'd never said anything about reciprocating her feelings because it made being around him harder to a large degree. The what-if was going to haunt her forever. Yes, she could give him time, and likely she would, but if he honestly believed he was cursed and intended to keep her at arm's length because of it, she would have a difficult time convincing him otherwise.

She decided then and there that this would be the last case they'd work on together. If Simon still felt the same way once his name was cleared, Evelyn would move on. Find something else to occupy her time. Maybe move to England and stay with Mackenzie for a while. Delaney needed a crazy old relative to spoil her rotten whenever her parents told her no.

"I can feel you thinking hard all the way over here." Simon peeked at her from under his arm. "Why the long face?"

"I suppose I should think more quietly," she replied in a teasing tone.

The leather of his sofa creaked lightly as he shifted to a sitting position. "Something bothering you about the case?"

He'd given her the perfect excuse, so she went with it. "Yes. I'm trying to work through why Pete chose you. He hired you, and even if he hated you—which he never gave an inkling of, by the way—as a director, he could've easily had you moved to another division. So why choose you for the carefully constructed setup?" She stood to pace, mainly to remove his bared chest from her line of sight so she didn't jump him like the sex-starved animal she was. "If I can under-stand that much, I can figure out the rest."

"Believe me, I've been asking the same questions." Simon sounded tired and completely out of sorts.

"Want to pick this back up tomorrow morning?" she asked kindly.

"Yeah, I suppose that's a good plan." He rose to his feet, stretched, then bent to pick up the empty glasses. His obsessive cleanliness habit saved his life.

One of the floor-to-ceiling panels of glass behind him shattered a millisecond before a vase exploded beside Evelyn. Their training kicked in, and they both dropped to the floor. Simon army-crawled to her side, and the two of them sought cover behind the sofa she'd been sitting on a minute before.

"Did you see where the shot came from?" he asked as he ran his hand under the sofa table to retrieve a Glock he'd hidden there.

"No, but if I had to guess based on the trajectory, I'd say the western wing of your complex, one floor up."

He snorted. "That's a damned precise guess."

A whoosh sounded as a bullet tore through the center of the sofa, followed by another. The second grazed Evelyn's arm, and she couldn't prevent her hiss of pain. She'd been shot once in the line of duty, and the sting of this more recent injury was nothing compared to that.

Without saying a word and acting on pure instinct, she gripped Simon's wrist and teleported them to her bedroom. The first thing he did when they landed was touch his hands to his chest. Then, he stared at her, wide-eyed and breathless.

"First teleport?" she asked, careful to keep her voice at a whisper.

He shook his head, eyes still locked on her. "It just felt different with you."

She winked, placed a finger to her lips, and tip-toed to the door of her bedroom.

Logic dictated that if there had been an attempted assassination of Simon, there was the likelihood of an attack on her. At work, she'd been the Watson to his Sherlock Holmes. Where Simon went, so did Evelyn, and vice versa. Pete knew it, and if he was truly behind this, he would anticipate her participation in an investigation, retired or not.

Just as she reached the door, the knob turned. Evelyn mouthed Granny Thorne's cloaking spell and waved her hands to encompass both Simon and herself.

"Only shift out of the way if our intruder looks like he is going to impact you directly, Simon," she said with a calmness she didn't feel as a stranger entered her bedroom. "We're hidden for the moment."

"He can't hear us?"

"No. The cloaking spell hides sight, sound, and smell. If we move fast, he could feel a light breeze of air, but otherwise it's like we're not here."

"Handy."

"Exceedingly." She pressed back against the wall to avoid collision with a man in head-to-toe black. Keeping an eye on his progress, she parted her shirt to quickly assess her wound. Writing it off as a scratch, she applied pressure against the puckered flesh and directed a healing light to knit the skin.

She needed to shift a second time as her intruder passed to check the closet. Next, he searched her dresser, pausing to lift a pair of silky panties and sniff them.

"Fucking pervert," Simon muttered.

Anger simmered in his voice, and the look of black rage on his visage was worrisome. Evelyn wouldn't put it past him to punch the guy on principle alone.

"It's just material, Simon Says," she reminded him. "No harm, no foul—for now." She waved him to her and gripped his hand in hers as the perp rifled through her nightstand. The man picked up a tanzanite ring Evelyn had been careless enough to leave there, and stuffed it in his pocket.

She grinned.

"What's so funny?" Simon asked.

His confusion made her chuckle.

"In less than sixty seconds, my cousin will arrive with his personal militia in tow."

"I don't understand."

"That ring creates a telepathic link from the wearer to the one who created it—Alastair Thorne."

Evelyn had told Simon enough about the family patriarch to make him wary. "But he's not wearing it."

"I should mention it's also enchanted to alert my cousin if it's handled by anyone other than who it was created for.

"Oh, shit."

She grinned again. "Exactly so."

CHAPTER 6

The air crackled—an indication of an incoming magical force—and grew so heavy that even Evelyn's panty-raiding burglar took note. He raised his head from ransacking her place and sniffed the air like a wild animal. Wide and wary, his gaze darted around the room, and some sixth sense had him lifting his gun to soothe the anxiety the sensation caused.

Simon felt the ripple across his skin and sent a side-glance toward Evelyn to see if she was similarly affected. He didn't have time to comment before three men, all garbed in military-like clothing with rifle butt pressed to shoulder and an eye staring down a scope, burst into the room followed by an elegantly dressed blond-haired man with a deceptively bored air and a sharp gaze.

The intruder had an oh-shit moment and pointed his gun at the seemingly easy target. "Tell them to back off, or I'll shoot," the guy yelled.

The newcomer, whom Simon assumed was Alastair Thorne, raised his brows and straightened his shirt cuffs. "By all means, *shoot.*"

Behind Alastair, a giant of a man with coffee-colored shoulder-length hair casually leaned his weight against the door jamb. "Dude.

Do you know what my prickly pear will do to me if you get shot? I'll be sleeping in the dog house for weeks."

"Stop whining like a little girl, Quentin. Holly knows well enough how irritating Al can be. She'd never hold it against you," one of other men replied.

Evelyn's snort somehow alerted Alastair to her presence, and he cast a furtive look in their direction.

"I thought you said we were undetectable," Simon whispered, just in case.

"We are. Alastair—the arrogant fucker in the middle there—is an empath. He can feel our presence and sense our emotions."

"Note to self, don't bother trying to play hide-and-seek with Alastair Thorne," Simon muttered.

Evelyn hugged his bicep and laughed. "You're a very smart man, Simon Says."

The trapped gunman pointed his weapon at one person then shifted it to another just as quickly, unsure who his target should be.

"Give it up, boy," Alastair said. "You can't escape unless it's in a body bag."

But damned if the guy didn't try!

He aimed and pulled the trigger.

The bullet stopped mid-flight and hung in the air until Quentin stepped forward and knocked it to the ground—much to Simon's shock and awe.

"Can you do that?" he demanded.

"Superman a bullet like Quentin?" She shook her head. "Nope. That's a special talent all his own."

"Fuck, that would be a useful ability to have."

Again, she laughed.

In seconds, the intruder was face down on the floor trussed up with zip ties, resembling a Thanksgiving turkey.

"We could've used these guys on our team," Simon said.

"They're too loyal to Alastair, and he is totally anti-establishment." Evelyn then spoke something in Latin. "Don't do anything awful like pick your nose, Simon Says. We're visible now."

"Thanks for the warning."

Alastair stepped forward with a wide, warm smile. "Hello, child."

"Hello, Cousin." Evelyn embraced him, then turned to hug one of the other men. "Ryker! It's good to see you, my friend."

"Notice how she's much happier to see me, Al? This goes back to you being an irritating ass," Ryker quipped.

Other than a droll look for Ryker, Alastair didn't respond. He held out the ring he'd retrieved from the intruder. "I believe this is yours."

Evelyn accepted it with a nod and slipped it into her pocket. "Thanks for the rescue."

"That's supposed to be worn to keep you out of danger, child."

"I'm not in danger right now." She gave him a cheeky grin and kissed his cheek. "I'll wear it when necessary. Promise."

"Fair enough." Alastair faced Simon. "And you must be Evelyn's boyfriend."

"Oh! Uh, no. Not… no." She blushed. "He's my ex-boss."

Other than cocking his head at a slight angle and shifting his gaze between the two of them, her cousin didn't respond.

"Simon Blane."

"Blane?" Alastair shook his hand with a frown. "Any relation to Benjamin or Trevor Blane?"

Uncomfortable discussing his dad with a stranger, Simon merely said, "Trevor's my older brother." He anticipated what would come next. People always questioned the fact his brother possessed magic, but Simon didn't. That was the thing with children of mixed magic families. Sometimes one child was blessed with abilities, and the other wasn't. Like his mother before him, Simon was born without gifts.

Alastair surprised him with a simple nod as if he was filing away the information for future reference.

Quentin stepped forward and swept Evelyn off her feet into a bear hug. "Good to see you again, you hawt thang."

"Hello, gorgeous."

Simon took exception.

"Put her down," he ordered, and the steel in his tone conveyed a don't-fuck-with-me command.

All present looked at him in surprise. Evelyn included.

Quentin was the first to recover, and his fading grin suddenly widened. Mischief danced in those dark, bedroom eyes that women seemed to treasure on a guy but that Simon hated.

"I thought he was only your ex-boss, hawt thang," he said in an aside to Evelyn as he set her on her feet. His gaze stayed locked on Simon as the two men summed each other up. "Seems he feels otherwise."

Simon stole a look at Evelyn and saw her bemusement begin to fade. A teasing light entered her blue eyes, and she crossed to where he stood. "What if I told you Quentin and I are running away together to—" she glanced back at the god-like creature "—where are we going again?"

"The Caribbean Islands," he supplied without hesitation. "My prickly pear will never find us there."

"Right." She looked straight at Simon. "What if I told you Quentin and I are running away together to the Caribbean Islands?"

"I'd say the hell you are." At the sight of her satisfied smile, Simon added, "We have to put Pete away before you go."

She socked him in the stomach.

CHAPTER 7

$\mathcal{E}$velyn vocally wished the laughing men to perdition and stomped straight to her kitchen. Simon joined her shortly thereafter.

"Sorry."

She turned to find him with his elbows resting on the counter and a contrite expression. She was taken aback to see his shirt still hung open. In all the excitement, she'd forgotten he was half-undressed. No wonder Alastair had assumed Simon was her boyfriend.

Turning her back to him, she removed eight coffee mugs from the cabinet and placed them on the granite countertop. "For what?"

"For teasing you."

She shrugged. "I started it."

"Actually, Quentin did, so we can blame him for your ill humor."

Evelyn smiled as she conjured steaming coffee for each cup. With a wiggle of her fingers, she made Simon's the way he liked it and slid the mug in front of him. "I have no ill humor happening."

"That punch to my gut said differently."

"That was just to remove the smug look from your face. I don't like it when people get the better of me."

"Don't I know it," he said and lifted the coffee cup to take a sip.

She leaned in and jabbed his chest with her fingertip. "And that punch was a love tap. It probably hurt my hand more than your rock-hard stomach."

Simon captured her finger and kissed the tip. "You're forgiven."

"Pfft. Whatever. Now button up your shirt so I can concentrate on the upcoming conversation. Alastair is going to want details." She was about to turn away when she remembered what she'd intended to ask. "Why didn't you tell me you had a brother, Simon?"

"I don't talk to him."

"Why not?" She'd known about his orphaned status, but she hadn't realized he had another sibling wandering around. For whatever reason, he'd purposely kept his brother's existence a secret, and she was curious why.

Simon shrugged, looked at the contents of his cup, and took another sip of coffee. His standard evasive move. He clearly had no intention of discussing Trevor Blane, and Evelyn would need to find another source for her information.

That source joined them at the counter not long after. "I need a word with you in private, child."

"I have no secrets from Simon."

Alastair's all-seeing sapphire eyes studied them both for a hot minute, no doubt taking note of Simon hastily buttoning his shirt. "Nevertheless, I want to speak to you alone. I'm not in the habit of airing family business in front of strangers."

"It's all right, Evelyn," Simon assured her with a hard look at Alastair. "But you should know, Mr. Thorne, this likely isn't a result of your 'family business' but of someone after me."

Rarely did one see Alastair flummoxed, and the confusion on his face was priceless. If she had her cellphone handy, Evelyn would've snapped a picture for the family album.

"We were at Simon's, and someone shot at us. We think we know who it's related to, but we don't have all the information. No what, or exact why yet," she explained.

Alastair gave a sharp nod. "Duly noted. Now come with me, child."

With a roll of her eyes for Simon's sake, she followed her cousin to the guest room. "Okay, what is so secretive you had to drag me away?"

"Do you know the Blane family history?"

She sobered and stilled. Although Alastair was the black sheep of the witch community, he was knowledgeable about all things magic related, and that included any family with abilities.

"I don't," she admitted.

"Considering what you used to do for a living, I'm surprised you never investigated your boss."

"I never needed to. I trust him," she retorted. And she'd never admit it, but she felt a little foolish now that he mentioned it. As a Thorne witch, she needed to be cautious and suspicious of everyone. Their enemies were plentiful.

"It wasn't a criticism, Evelyn," he said gently. "I'm an untrusting old fool, and I assume everyone else is the same."

"No offense taken. So what do I need to know?"

"The Blanes are Death Dealers."

She didn't know what the hell that was, but it didn't sound good. She said as much.

Alastair gave her a put-upon look. "Your generation's magical knowledge is sorely lacking. Remind me to give your parents a stern talking to."

"After this is over, you can have at it." His chuckle soothed Evelyn's overactive nerve endings. There was something about Alastair's cool command that had a way of putting everyone around him at ease. She circled her hand for him to continue. "Now, what's a Death Dealer?"

"Exactly what it sounds like. They are the takers of life. Most are employed by the Authority to maintain balance."

Maintain balance? Balance of what?

"What the hell does that mean?" she demanded.

"When a person cheats death, they create a cosmic imbalance. It throws off Fate's design. The Authority will hire the Blanes of the witch world to come in and right that wrong."

"You're saying Simon is a Death Dealer?"

"I'd be surprised if he isn't. There is a darkness hanging over him."

"The curse," she mumbled, thinking back to what he'd said.

"Curse?"

Not ready to go there yet, Evelyn waved a hand in dismissal. "Just something Simon said."

"You don't want to be involved with one, child. It will bring certain death."

"What?" She felt the blood drain from her head, and she swayed in place. *Had Simon been unknowingly telling the truth?*

Alastair reached out a hand to steady her. "You love him already," he said flatly.

Unable to speak past the constriction in her throat, she nodded.

"I see," he murmured.

Her cousin's troubled expression ratcheted up Evelyn's anxiety.

"What?" she croaked. "What do you see? What am I missing?"

Drawing her into a tight hug, Alastair pressed his cheek to the top of her head. "You'll be fine, child. I guarantee it."

"I don't know how you can guarantee anything in light of what you just revealed."

"We're Thornes. Even the Fates prefer not to tangle with us if they can help it."

Evelyn snorted a laugh and hugged him tighter. "Thank you, Alastair. You should know, Simon and I really are just friends, though. He's still in love with his deceased wife." She went cold the moment the words left her mouth. "Tiffany!"

If Simon was indeed cursed, and if he had suspected he was prior to Tiffany's death, it made him a shitty person. But Evelyn found it hard to reconcile the caring man she knew with the one it would make him, had he known what he was capable of.

If anyone could get a bead on Simon's thoughts, it would be her cousin, though. "Alastair, do you think she could've possibly known what he was and still stayed? And how could he be so unfeeling? To be with her, knowing it would end her life?"

But he didn't answer; instead, his attention was caught by something beyond her shoulder. She spun around to see Simon, red-faced and trembling with rage.

"What the hell are you talking about?"

CHAPTER 8

*S*imon was furious.

His curiosity was piqued, and he'd decided to seek out the Thornes, only to overhear Evelyn ask how he could be callous enough to have a relationship with Tiffany. Or at least he *assumed* Evelyn had been referring to him.

"I think you need to clarify your statement—*immediately.*"

Trepidation was in her eyes, and she darted a look between him and Alastair.

Apprehension filled Simon. What was it she thought he'd done? He hated her uneasy look. Never, in all the years they'd known each other, had she looked at him with something other than friendship or respect. Needing to get to the bottom of her sudden suspicion, he joined them inside the room. "Spit it out, Evelyn."

"Why didn't you tell me you were a Death Dealer?" she blurted in one rushed sentence.

"Because I'm not," he snapped, startled by her aggression. "I don't even know what that is."

Alastair seemed taken aback. "Your father and your brother both possess that power, Mr. Blane. The ability to end a life with a mere touch. It's your legacy."

"What? No!" The shock Simon experienced sent him reeling backward a few steps, and he shook his head in disbelief. "No. You're wrong. My father died when I was six, and Trev… Trev…" But what was Trevor other than absent? He had been for most of Simon's adult life. How would he even know what abilities his brother possessed?

Simon sat—or rather slid—down on his ass with his back against the wall.

"I have no abilities," he said tiredly, closing his eyes.

"It's true," he heard Evelyn say after a pregnant pause. "Or none that I've seen. He's never used magic since I've known him."

"Interesting. It seems we need to speak to your family to find out who bound your powers, Mr. Blane. Because by all accounts, you should have them."

Alastair's comment caught Simon's full attention. *What?*

"Your mother was a full-blooded witch, and your father was a Death Dealer. And, as I said, unless your magic was bound, you should possess abilities. Powerful ones at that."

He could barely process the fact he might've had magic once, but he'd always believed his mother had been without. Not that he could remember anyone saying it in so many words.

"Jesus!"

"I suggest you get Trevor here. The sooner, the better," Evelyn said in a shaky but determined voice. "We can deal with the Pete Wilson problem later."

"Actually, I think the most important issue is the latter," Alastair said. "As such, we'll all relocate to my estate." He stopped any potential objections by saying, "I'd rather not leave you here, running back and forth like little metal ducks in a shooting gallery. It's not safe for either of you."

Evelyn approached Simon and gave him an apologetic look. Words didn't need to be spoken between them. Their special bond after all these years allowed for small disagreements. He couldn't say her brand of distrust didn't hurt, but he could understand it.

"I doubt anyone would attack us a third time in one night. But just in case, I intend to see what the asshat in the next room has to say."

Alastair held up a hand to halt her. "Ryker and Quentin are interrogating him. If there's anything to discover, they will."

"I'm not used to letting other people clean up my messes, cuz, so you'll forgive me if I want to be present." With that bit of attitude, she stalked from the room.

Simon snorted and suppressed a laugh.

Goddess, he loved her feistiness.

"Let's go drink the coffee Evelyn was kind enough to prepare," Alastair suggested. "It will give you time to decide what you want to say to your brother and father."

"My father is dead, Mr. Thorne. You're mistaken if you believe otherwise."

"I hate to be the one to break it to you, son, but I spoke to Ben less than six months ago. Unless he died within that window of time, he's still alive." Although the words were spoken in a kind tone, they still hit Simon with the full force of a sledgehammer.

"Are you fucking kidding me?" He surged to his feet and began pacing. "Thirty-seven years! For *thirty-seven years,* I've believed... I thought... he... *Fuck!* Are you sure?"

"Come on. Let's see if we can solve this particular mystery."

The compassion on the other man's face nearly took Simon out at the knees. He remembered a similar look on his father's face the last night they'd spoken. Benjamin Blane had been a superhero in Simon's young eyes. Hell, he'd held that status for most of Simon's adult life too.

His father. *Alive!*

Every type of emotion bombarded him: anger, bitterness, hope, hatred, love, confusion—all warring for dominance. The burning question was *why?*

Simon reached into his pocket, prepared to whip out his cellphone, only to realize he'd left it back at his place. He swore and rubbed a hand along the back of his neck. It would be great to be able to teleport back and get it. As the thought occurred to him, he froze. He met Alastair's watchful gaze.

"You said you believed I've been bound. How can we find that out?"

"We'd need to speak to the people with the power to do it."

"A regular witch couldn't?"

"No. I doubt even I would be strong enough on my own. It would take someone like Benjamin and your brother, Trevor, working in conjunction, or a higher power like the Authority."

"The Authority. I feel like I've heard that term before, but I can't recall when or where."

"The Authority is an organization a step above the Witches' Council. They balance the scales, so to speak. They recruit those witches with the most unique powers to carry out their wishes. The Authority is ruled by the Fates."

"I have so many questions, but I'm not sure I could process any more information right now." He laced his fingers together behind his neck and gave a small shake of his head.

He'd always known magic existed, but he never cared much. Other than the rare times they stumbled across a criminal misusing their abilities, he'd never truly had to deal with anything associated with the witch community. Evelyn was his go-to person for things of that nature, and he'd been happy to let her do it. The Authority didn't sound like any organization he'd care to be a member of.

"You think my father would've worked for them?"

"I know he did."

"And Trev, too?"

"I believe so, yes."

"Let's forgo the coffee. I think I need something stronger."

"Evelyn keeps a bottle of Glenfiddich on hand for me."

Simon laughed, completely surprised he could. "She told me that was for me."

"She's a wily one, our Evelyn."

As they walked down the hall to the kitchen, Simon mulled over what he'd overheard when he first approached the Thornes. Evelyn wasn't one to overreact, and the horrified supposition in her voice struck Simon right in the heart. But he couldn't dismiss her base fear, which was now his. "She thinks I'm the reason for Tiffany's death, doesn't she?"

"I can't attest to what is in Evelyn's mind, son."

"But she asked you—" he swallowed down his sudden grief and tried again "—she asked you how I could be with Tiff knowing I would bring her death. Is that what I did? Are all Death Dealers cursed?"

CHAPTER 9

lastair sighed. How had the previous generations failed the newer generations so badly? At a time when instant communication was handy, no one bothered to have an informative conversation or give instruction. And someone with the power of a Death Dealer should never be left to wander around blindly. If the one who'd bound Simon's powers died suddenly, the young man would come into abilities with the power to devastate the lives of everyone he knows. As it was, Alastair suspected there was residual magic lingering within Simon; otherwise, the dark aura wouldn't be surrounding him.

As he poured the scotch into tumblers, he glanced at the romantic little tree sitting in the corner of the living room. He hadn't missed the yearning on Evelyn's face whenever she looked at Simon. The girl was in for heartache if Alastair couldn't find a way to level the magical playing field.

"Tell me about your wife, Blane. How long were you married, and how did she die?"

The abrupt question surprised Simon, and confusion heaped with a whole host of anger built inside the man. Alastair could feel the conflicting energy like a sharp slap, and with a wave of his hand, he quickly put into place a magical barrier against whatever residual magic could harm him. He made a mental note to instruct Evelyn on how to do it. Her parents had likely never told her how.

"My marriage is none of your damned business," Simon said.

"I would think, as an FBI supervisor and agent, you'd be inclined to think before reacting, son."

A deep frown drew Simon's brows together, and after a moment, he compressed his lips and nodded. "You'd be right. I'm sensitive on the subject of Tiffany."

"I'm sorry for your loss."

"Thanks."

Simon downed the alcohol like a college boy at a frat party, and Alastair winced.

"That's no way to appreciate Glenfiddich, boy."

For the first time, Simon let down his guard completely. And when the other man grinned, Alastair could see why Evelyn was attracted to him. In that instant, Simon became engaging and approachable. A very different man from his father or brother.

"Normally, I'd agree with you, Mr. Thorne, but I needed the effects to take hold right away."

"You're forgiven."

They shared a smile and drank in companionable silence for a few minutes. Simon was the first to speak.

"I met Tiffany when I was fourteen. It was two months before my aunt was killed."

"I'm assuming she was a classmate of yours?"

"Yes. Aunt Alice insisted I stop seeing Tiff. She told me I'd end up with a broken heart, and my kind shouldn't mix with hers."

"I have an idea what she meant, but more importantly, do you?"

Simon shook his head. "At the time, I thought she was being a snob. My family came from money, and Tiff's didn't."

"But now?"

"Well, thanks to what I found out today, I suspect she had a different motive."

"That's what I believe, too. When and how did your wife die?"

"Roughly three years ago, she developed an inoperable brain tumor. After a year-long fight, she passed away."

"Did you seek a magical alternative?"

"Evelyn did. She tried everything she could think to do. Healers, spells, the works."

"So she bought your wife time but couldn't heal her."

Simon looked up sharply. "What do you mean?"

"I suspect your Tiffany would've passed away much sooner had Evelyn not stepped in." Alastair's pride in his cousin swelled. A Thorne only truly loved once, and it stood to reason that Evelyn recognized her feelings for Simon early on. Based on what Alastair had just learned, she selflessly acted to save Simon's wife and preserve the man's happiness.

"I never thought about it. I—"

Simon looked up, but Alastair didn't need to turn to see who had entered the room. The longing on the man's face said exactly who stood behind him.

These two are like star-crossed lovers, he thought wryly. Neither was able to see the forest for the trees. If they could get out of their own way long enough to have a serious conversation, they'd find they were on the same page.

"Evelyn, dear, we were just discussing you," Alastair said, hiding a smile with a sip of scotch. "Do join us for this interesting discussion."

"Another of your cat-and-mouse games, Al?" Ryker asked dryly from somewhere behind him.

Evelyn snorted and walked to Simon's side of the counter. Alastair didn't miss the way she touched the man's shoulder in comfort or the way Simon's attention remained focused on her as she prepared a meat-and-cheese tray for the others.

"So, why are you toying with Simon, cuz?" she asked. "Tell us what you suspect and be done with it."

"Always to the point, aren't you?" Alastair straightened his cuffs, hiked up his slacks, and sat down at the table. He didn't wait for her to answer and instead asked, "What sources did you use to prolong Tiffany's life, child?"

She didn't pause in preparing the food, and after she placed the tray in the center of the table, she waved Simon over. "Come eat. You barely consume enough to stay alive."

"You're not my mother, Evelyn. Stop acting like it." Simon's tone was packed with exasperation.

Sexual frustration, if Alastair wasn't mistaken.

"She can't help it," Ryker said. "Our family eats in a crisis. It's what we do."

Evelyn smiled, took a long drink of her coffee, then answered Alastair's original question. "Spring was kind enough to give me herbs from her garden. GiGi walked me through the spell. Since Tiff was a mortal, I had to be careful and a little clandestine." Evelyn cast a side look at Simon when he clasped her hand, and Alastair watched her blink away tears. "I'm sorry I couldn't save her for you, Simon," she choked out.

"You did everything you could." He leaned in and kissed her temple. "Thank you."

"It wasn't enough."

One didn't have to be an empath to feel her anguish.

Alastair silently debated his next reveal but ultimately decided he needed to share. "You prolonged her life, child, but she was going to die either way. That was what Alice was trying to tell you, Blane. It had nothing to do with whether Tiffany's family came from money or whether she was dirt poor."

"I really am cursed, aren't I?" Simon asked somberly.

"Yes."

CHAPTER 10

$\mathcal{E}$velyn didn't know what to think or feel in the face of Alastair's revelation.

Simon was cursed.

The idea was unthinkable, and yet, he'd suspected the truth before now. Had even mentioned it to her earlier in the evening. She'd poohpoohed the idea as hogwash, but now, she couldn't argue the point. Any relationship between them was doomed, either to never exist or to be her untimely death.

She looked down at their clasped hands. They were both whiteknuckling it, and each held the other like a lifeline. It provided a truer insight into Simon's feelings than anything else ever had. He really did love her. If he didn't, he wouldn't be as upset as he was. Outwardly, he didn't show a thing. But his stillness was telling, as was the death grip on her hand.

"We don't accept that," she heard herself say. "*I* don't accept that." She locked eyes with Simon. In his, she saw frustration backed by resignation. "I don't, Simon. You shouldn't either."

He dropped his gaze to their joined hands and very carefully withdrew his.

Rejection, in any form, stung, and Evelyn experienced that sickening sensation of her heart dropping into her stomach.

"Right," she said softly, cradling her mug to draw on its heat. The sudden coldness in her soul wasn't likely to be offset by the warm ceramic, but she was willing to try anything to not feel so leaden and chilled. "Well, that's a problem for another day." She took a sip of her coffee to establish some normalcy. "Ryker and Quentin didn't get anywhere with the jerk-off in the bedroom. Either he doesn't know anything, or he's a hell of an employee."

Thankfully, the others jumped on the conversation wagon.

"She's correct," Ryker stated. "The guy is tight-lipped. I'm leaning toward uninformed. Could be he was hired through back channels and doesn't know who is in charge."

"And he's mortal," Evelyn added with a nod. It always annoyed her when the magical beings pulled the unknowing into messes of this nature. Granted, the guy was sent to assassinate her, or at the very least, rough her up, but if whoever hired him had abilities, then they had to know there was a good chance their guy would never succeed against her power.

"Is your Pete Wilson mortal as well?" Ryker asked as he slapped together a ham and cheese hoagie.

"Before today, I'd have said yes," Simon replied. "I've never noticed the tell-tale glow to indicate otherwise. Have you, Evelyn?"

"No. And maybe that's why he sent one after us. He might not know what we are."

Ryker paused before taking a bite of his food. "Ever hear the name before, Al?"

"Can't say that I have."

"So, our general consensus is that Pete isn't of magical descent." Evelyn handed a napkin to Ryker and gestured to the mayo on his beard with a wry smile. "We need to wipe this guy's memory before we turn him loose."

Simon's head whipped in her direction. "What? He's not going to be turned loose. He attacked two FBI agents."

"No, he attacked one retired agent and a suspended one. It's doubtful anyone is going to care because they believe we're dirty."

"Evelyn, this is proof that we aren't."

"What part of *Pete set you up* don't you get, Simon?" she asked, none too nicely. He had to understand the rules didn't apply here. "Even if we did this by the book, we would need hard evidence, and this guy isn't it. He doesn't know who hired him."

"I'm inclined to agree with Evelyn," Ryker said. "This isn't a by-the-book situation."

Simon frowned. "She didn't say it wasn't."

Sitting back in his chair, Alastair crossed his arms. "Didn't she, though?"

"Simon, we have to do this the Thorne way. We have the magical means to stop Pete and restore your career. Any other way, and we're running around in the dark, completely helpless. We won't know when another attack is coming." Evelyn met his stormy gaze and shrugged. "I asked you earlier, and you seemed okay with whatever we needed to do to clear this up."

"Yes, but I don't agree with putting murderers back on the streets, and that's what you are suggesting we do here."

She looked at Alastair for help, silently handing off the argument to him. He gave a subtle nod.

"We've delayed here long enough," Alastair said. "I'll take you two back to my place, and we can leave Ryker and Quentin to clean up this mess."

Pausing with the last of his sandwich halfway to his mouth, Ryker frowned. "Why am I always cleaning up the messes?"

Alastair grinned. "Because you're so good at it."

With a distinct "fuck you" and a gesture of his middle finger, Ryker rose to his feet, then dusted off his shirt and hands. He muttered to himself all the way back down the hall, much to his best friend's amusement.

"Poor Ryker. You need to treat him and GiGi to an all-expenses-paid trip somewhere, cuz." Evelyn said as she watched Simon clean up what remained of Ryker's little mess.

A rusty bark of laughter was Alastair's response. "He lives for things of this nature."

"Mmhmm. Well, be sure to tell him that, won't you?"

"Gather what you need, child. We should get going soon."

"I left my purse and the file at Simon's place. I'll need to teleport back to get those."

"Not alone, you're not."

"You think the sniper is still hanging out?" she asked in disbelief. "I find it highly doubtful after this long."

"Quentin will take you there to get what you need, but you'll do so under a cloaking spell." His stern look was intimidating as hell, and although Alastair was a teddy bear in most cases, there were still the rare occasions when he was not to be defied, like now.

CHAPTER 11

$\mathcal{E}$velyn and Simon returned to his apartment under the watchful eye of Quentin. A flirt and a seemingly good-time guy, Quentin knew when to be serious and was handy to have in a fight. He'd once told Evelyn that he owed her. The way he'd explained it was too convoluted for her brain to follow, but as a Traveler, Quentin could jump through and manipulate time. Apparently, in another timeline, she'd saved her cousin Holly heartache by putting a potential murderer behind bars, thereby allowing Quentin and Holly to be happy in this one.

Evelyn had accepted the praise because it came with a tight hug and Quentin's appreciation, and who didn't want *that*?

They waited in the corner of Simon's living room until Quentin gave them the all-clear to start gathering their things. As she shoved her file into her oversized bag, he checked locks and studied the trajectory of the bullets. Simon came from the bedroom with a black duffle stuffed to the brim, and Evelyn smiled at his apparent need to overpack.

"One of us could conjure whatever you need, Simon Says. You didn't need to bring everything but the kitchen sink."

"Shut it, Thorne. There are things I need."

"You're such a girl." She handed him his cell phone along with a duplicate one Alastair had given her. "My cousin said you need to upload your contacts and ditch the old one. He won't allow anything traceable in his home. It makes him too vulnerable to a strike against him."

"What about yours?"

"Already done while you were packing for a month."

Quentin shot them a sharp look from his place by the window. "Can you two hurry it up? This place makes my left ass cheek itch. I feel like we are moments away from attack."

Evelyn put a lot of stock into whatever powerful warlocks like Quentin felt. If he was concerned, then things just got real. "I'm ready to blow this joint. Simon?"

"Yep."

But before they could teleport, they received company.

The man was, without a doubt, related to Simon. The sandy-brown hair and piercing blue eyes were a dead giveaway, as was his haughty arrogance. Evelyn had seen Simon sporting the same disdainful and dismissive look on those rare occasions when it was warranted.

"Trevor?" Simon said with a great deal of shock.

"He can't hear you. You're cloaked," Quentin reminded him. "And before you ask, I'm not removing it."

Evelyn slapped the back of her hand against Quentin's rock-hard abs and immediately regretted it. Her knuckles felt like they came in contact with granite. As she shook out her hand, she said, "You know you don't need to remove it, Q. You only have to extend it to include Trevor."

"What if he's here to harm you? Alastair will cut off my head and spit down my windpipe if anything happens to you."

The visual was too much, and she laughed. "No, he won't. That's too undignified. He'd have his head of security or Ryker do it."

"Cut it out, you two. Trev is here for a reason, and I need to know why." Simon raised his brows and stared down Quentin—not an easy thing to do to a guy that was six-six and who was descended from Zeus.

"It's your neck on the chopping block, man." With a shrug, Quentin spoke the words to allow Trevor access to them.

"You don't seem surprised to see us here," Evelyn said to him.

"I'm not." He held up his hand to show a bandaged finger. "Blood tracking spell. Tells me exactly where my little brother is at all times."

She cast a side glance at Simon to see what he thought of his brother's comment. He didn't look thrilled.

The two men—similar in build, features, and coloring—stared at one another for a long minute. Surprisingly, it was Trevor who softened first. His eyes warmed, and he smiled as he held open his arms. "Hey, Si."

They embraced.

An ache started in Evelyn's chest and built as she recalled Simon's self-imposed isolation since his wife's death. He wouldn't reach out to anyone. Not her. Not his brother. Not any other friends that she knew of. He'd purposely closed himself off, and she suspected she knew why: *the curse.*

On the heels of her sadness came anger. How had Trevor left Simon to fend for himself without an explanation of what he was or what he was capable of? She opened her mouth to comment, only to have Simon give a subtle shake of his head. His uncanny ability to guess what she was thinking was downright disturbing at times.

She glared.

His mouth twitched as if he were fighting a grin.

His humor in tough or sticky situations was one of the things she liked about him the best. Yes, he was all business when it warranted, and he tended to be routinely more somber than her. However, he did have a lovely ability to laugh at himself.

Evelyn narrowed her eyes and crossed her arms in mock frustration. Simon lost the fight and revealed a dazzling grin—one that made her knees weak and her heart flutter. "We are on borrowed time, fellas. I think Trevor should say what he came here to say, so we can get moving," she said in a firm tone as she attempted to hide the heart on her sleeve.

"Let me talk to my brother for a few minutes, then we'll go," Simon assured her.

Quentin didn't look thrilled, but he gave a single nod and continued surveillance of the exterior landscape and adjoining buildings.

"Hurry, Simon. Every second we delay makes us sitting ducks. The family reunion can happen another time," she said.

As she walked to the other side of the living room, she paused in front of Tiffany's smiling picture. Like everyone, her friend hadn't been perfect or the model wife, but she'd loved her husband completely. Same with Simon. The two of them had been a delightful couple. Evelyn couldn't hope to compete with the memory of so stellar a relationship, and she wouldn't try. She was vastly different from his first wife and could never fit into the sweet, delicate mold. If whatever curse binding him could be broken and if he decided to take the journey with her, then she would do her best to make him happy. Once again, she told herself whatever happened, whatever the final outcome, she'd be okay.

CHAPTER 12

"Why didn't you tell me you were a Death Dealer, Trev? That Dad was still alive?" Simon was still reeling from the unexpected news, and the feeling of betrayal didn't sit well with him.

Trevor looked nonplussed for the span of a few heartbeats. "Dad's alive?"

"Are you going to try to convince me you didn't know?" Simon asked with pure disbelief. "Seriously? Because you both work for the same agency—the Authority—and I find it hard to believe you wouldn't have run across him by now."

"I *do* work for the Authority, Si. But I've never once seen our father. I've come in contact with other Dealers from time to time, but never him."

Simon studied his brother, looking for any hint of a lie or insincerity. He couldn't find either. Deciding to address the second issue, he asked, "Do you know who bound my powers?"

A cagey look flashed across Trevor's visage but disappeared just as quickly. He cast a wary glance toward the others as if he expected they were spies for the enemy. Finally, he sighed heavily. "I don't have proof, but I think perhaps it was the Authority."

"Why would they do that?"

"Most Dealers don't have more than one child. Two beings able to wield death in the family are usually considered acceptable. Three, not so much. One of us had to be neutralized, and since you were the youngest, it was you."

"And if Dad were to truly die? Would they then decide it's acceptable to give me back my natural-born gifts?" Simon asked with a bite to his tone.

"I don't know. They're a secretive lot."

"But it spills over, doesn't it?"

Trevor didn't pretend to misunderstand. He had to damn well know power like theirs couldn't be one-hundred-percent contained. Eventually, it bled over, and whoever was unfortunate enough to be in their lives would face a brutal death unless the Dealer retained the power to heal. Simon hadn't. "Yes. For you, it spills over," he acknowledged.

The regret shone in his brother's weary blue eyes, and Simon wanted to howl his rage. "How could you let me form a relationship, Trev? How could you let me marry Tiff knowing she was going to die so horribly?"

"You had twenty years, Si. It's more than some people."

"But she died! It wasn't like she divorced me and moved on with her life. She *died!*" His hands began to shake, and he wanted nothing more than to wipe the sympathetic expression from his brother's fucking face.

"Would you rather spend your life alone?"

"Yes, goddamn you!" he shouted. "I'd rather live alone than subject another person to that pain or myself to the torture of watching them die while I stood by and did nothing."

"I'm sorry, little brother. Truly."

Simon lifted his head and caught Evelyn's concerned gaze across the room. "If I stay with her, I'll kill her, too."

Trevor followed his line of sight. "Yes."

"What about you, Trev? Will it happen to whoever you love?"

Undecipherable emotion flashed in Trevor's eyes. "I won't, fall in love that is. I'm not built that way, and I've seen too much."

"You didn't answer my question."

"I don't believe it would happen to whoever I loved. I come equipped with the ability to heal."

Simon sagged back and sat on the edge of the sofa back.

"Brief affairs are your best option, Si. One-night stands. A week or two of play at the most."

"Fuck you if you think I'm putting what amounts to a poisoned dick into another victim."

Trevor stuttered an incredulous laugh. "You're going to live like a monk? Doubtful. Especially not with a hot piece of ass like her hanging around."

Blind fury ruled Simon's actions. One moment he was sitting; the next, his fist had connected with his brother's sneering face.

"Whatdefuck?" Trevor screamed as he bent over and cradled his now-crooked and quickly swelling nose. "I didn't think you'd *hit* me!"

"Never talk about her like that again. *Ever.*" Simon's steely tone promised retribution should Trevor disobey his edict.

His brother looked at him in disgust and no little pain. "I was testing your feelings for her, and it looks like you've fallen hard—*again.*" Trevor tilted his head back to stem the flow of blood. "You can't be with her, Si. Despite the fact she's a Thorne, she won't be strong enough."

"I know." And Simon felt the grief down to his soul. With Tiffany, he hadn't been aware he was to blame. If he caused Evelyn's eventual death knowing what he now did, he'd never be able to live with the guilt.

"Okay. Just so you do."

His brother's sympathetic expression was too much, and Simon avoided looking at him. Once again, he sought Evelyn, and once again, she was watching them, this time with shocked wonder. The desperate need to hold her, to absorb her into him completely, to protect her and love her, nearly brought him to his knees. But he couldn't have her.

He mentally shoved it all away. Shoved *her* away.

"First things first, I have to bring down Pete Wilson and stop the nameless assassins he's sent after me."

Trev zeroed in on Simon's internal sorrow. "While you're alive, there is always hope."

Any argument would be a waste of breath at this point. Simon had to remove Evelyn from Pete's radar and bring that sonofabitch down. Then he could figure out his miserable excuse of a life.

Quentin appeared next to them a moment later. "If you two are done with your little skirmish, we have to go. The feel of this place is off."

"How so?"

"I—"

An explosion rocked the door, cutting off his explanation.

CHAPTER 13

Chapter Thirteen has been omitted for obvious reasons. Consider this intermission. Feel free to take a bathroom break or get a cup of coffee. Your story will resume momentarily.

"Don't move," Quentin shouted.

But the blast had thrown Evelyn to the ground, and Simon was already in motion, determined to get to her. There was no way he wouldn't, not when her safety was of the utmost importance to him. As he squatted beside her, he noticed the trickle of blood down one temple. Frantically, he searched for a pulse; her wrist, her neck, then his ear to her heart. He couldn't feel or hear anything over his own pounding pulse. Just as he was about to lose his fucking mind, her arm lifted, and her fingers curled around the back of his head.

His breath whooshed out in his relief.

"I'm okay, Simon." She gave him one quick caress, then removed her hand. "We've got to move, or we'll be trampled."

The sound of booted feet running in the hallway hit him just as the first two agents breached the doorway. As one, Simon and Evelyn scrambled up and hastily backed closer to where Quentin and Trevor stood.

"What the fuck have you gotten yourself into, Brother?" Trevor asked when the remaining seven men burst through the opening.

"Serious shit by the looks of it," Quentin muttered. "Tell me you have what you need, and let's blow this popsicle stand."

"Yeah, I've got it. Evelyn?"

"Yep. Purse and file in hand," she replied with an aborted nod and a hiss of pain. Her hand flew to her neck. "I guess that fall hurt worse than I thought."

With great care, Simon drew her against him. "Are you sure you're okay?"

"We'll get her checked out first thing when we get back to Alastair," Quentin assured him.

Simon nodded as he loped the strap on his bag over his head. "Trev? You in?"

"Yeah. You never needed to ask."

They all touched hands, and Quentin made quick work of teleporting them back to Evelyn's place.

Their group wasn't there a second before Ryker urged them to relocate due to the large influx of federal agents about to storm the building. In no time at all, they were all standing within the walled garden just outside Alastair's palatial home.

"Trevor Blane," Alastair said casually. To Simon, there seemed to be a whole wealth of menace in the delivery of the name.

"Mr. Thorne," Trevor acknowledged respectfully.

The two men summed each other up. Alastair was the first to break the silent staring contest. "Find a way to rein in your power while in my home, Mr. Blane. If anyone so much as gets a sore throat, you'll answer to me."

A muscle ticked in Trevor's jaw, and he narrowed his eyes on the patriarch of the Thorne family. "I can give life just as easily as I can take it."

In the shock of seeing his brother and finding out the possibility his father was still alive, Simon had failed to register Trev's earlier comment regarding healing.

It finally sunk in.

"You could've cured Tiff?" A wary look crossed his brother's face, and Simon wanted to beat him to a pulp because he knew that look.

He knew that Trevor was about to prevaricate or dodge to save his ass. "Answer the question, Trev."

"I don't know if I could have." Trevor finally said with a grimace. "I didn't find out about Tiffany's illness until it was well established. But the Authority was adamant that I not step in. The Fates believed there was something bigger at play."

The day had been one constant barrage of information after another, and Simon's standard ability to calmly deal was giving way to his temper. He'd always been a thinker and tended not to be reactive if he could help it. Today, however, had stretched him beyond his limits.

"Fuck the Authority! And fuck you, Trevor!" Simon's emotions were all over the place, but the predominant feeling was bitterness. His brother had failed him. When he needed help the most, Simon was left to flounder, and his wife died because of it.

Knowing there was nothing he could do to heal Evelyn's superficial wound, Simon left her in Alastair's capable hands and took off for the woods bordering the property. He needed time to process everything he'd learned in the last few hours, and he couldn't be around his brother without committing murder.

He'd given no thought to the hour or the darkness when he left the house, but he greatly appreciated that the illuminated pathway provided by subtle lighting, not dissimilar to a nightlight or garden lights, for him to find his way. Where these particular ones originated from was anyone's guess. For all he knew at this point, faeries existed in the enchanted woods surrounding him. Nothing would surprise him now.

It felt like he'd walked for hours, but it was probably more like minutes when he came upon a glade. This, too, was illuminated, although not as brightly as the trail. In the center of the clearing was a flat stone altar, about seven feet in length and roughly three-feet wide. Unsure what force drove him, he laid down on the smooth surface and stared up at the midnight sky. Ultra-bright stars twinkled and took turns winking at him. As a young kid, Simon had wondered if that was where his mother and father existed after death. He eventually learned about the Otherworld and the existence of multiple planes where souls dwelled to either be reborn or retired forever.

Would Tiff choose to reincarnate?

It was the one thing they'd never discussed. Mainly because of her upbringing.

"Simon."

Evelyn's gentle, caring voice drifted to him. Of course, she would seek him out. It's what she did, part of her usual M.O. When things were wrong, she needed to set them to rights.

He closed his eyes against the mental fatigue he was experiencing. "What is it, Evelyn?"

Her voice sounded closer when she said, "You seemed in a… fragile state back there. I wanted to be sure you were okay."

"I'm not."

She stopped beside the altar but didn't touch him, and for that, he was grateful. In his mind, he had the past, present, and future all tangled up with his feelings, and he didn't know how to wade through the sea of emotions.

"For what it's worth, your brother feels wretched."

Simon lifted his lids in time to see her place her palms flat on the altar and hoist herself into a sitting position. Her profile was to him as she stared out over the clearing. The calm, collected manner in which she spoke irritated him.

"I don't give a shit how Trevor feels. He's a liar and a coward. He could've saved Tiffany."

Evelyn's mouth tightened into a thin line as she nodded.

"You disagree?" He asked challengingly, spoiling for a fight to get rid of his excess energy and anger.

"I don't know anything about his abilities or what should've been yours, Simon Says. I just know that he is between a rock and a hard place. He cares about you, but he's contracted with the Authority."

"So?"

"According to Alastair, to go against them is to court your own death." Evelyn finally looked down at him. "Would you have preferred your brother be executed for disobeying the rules and for you to lose Tiffany anyway? Because that's what would've happened."

"Stop being so goddamned logical all the time," Simon grumbled.

Evelyn's full lips twitched. "I'll try not to annoy you with reason in the future." She knocked her knuckles against his hip. "Scoot over. I want to lie down."

He edged to his right to make room for her, and he welcomed what little warmth she offered when she curled into him. The February night was frigid, and in all the hoopla, he'd failed to grab a coat.

"You and I can never be permanent, Evelyn. I'm not going to risk your life."

"Why don't you let me worry about myself, Simon Says. You have enough on your plate."

A surge of heat flooded his body as her hand settled on the center of his chest. Magical warmth, she'd called it once when they were on a stakeout. She could warm a body with a single touch if she chose to. "How did you know I was cold?"

"It's the middle of February, in the North Carolina mountains, in the early hours. I'd be worried about you if you weren't cold."

A smile curled his lips, and he couldn't stop himself from kissing the crown of her head. "Thanks."

"Don't mention it."

They lay in silence, staring up at the stars for what felt like an hour. Finally, he spoke. "I suppose we should go back."

"You sound reluctant," she murmured softly as if she was drowsy.

"I am. Returning means we have to deal with all the things."

He felt her shrug. "Not tonight. We go back, get a good night's sleep, and deal with 'all the things' in the morning after breakfast."

"You don't think Pete will send anyone else tonight?"

Evelyn snorted a laugh. "I'd bet my trust fund Pete wouldn't find us in a hundred years. Not here." She shifted to one elbow and gazed down at Simon. "This is Thorne land, and the wards are impenetrable. At least from the Pete Wilson's of the world."

The moonlight glinted off of Evelyn's honey-gold hair and bathed her skin in its glow. Simon suddenly didn't care about the rest of the world or curses or anything but her and her achingly beautiful face.

"I do love you, Evelyn Thorne. Despite what may happen after this moment, you should know that with your unconditional friendship, you have always been my true north."

CHAPTER 15

$\mathcal{E}$velyn wasn't quite sure what to say. On the one hand, she wanted to scoff at the word friendship, but she couldn't. They *were* friends—the very best—and if she paused to analyze it, she'd have to admit he had always been her true north as well. But dammit, she hated that he kept shoving her into the friend zone. She wanted to be so much more.

Which brought her to the other hand. The moonlight loved his face, loved the planes of his high cheekbones and the sharp, chiseled jawline. Almost as much as she did. The temptation to kiss him, to show him what he would be missing in life, was strong.

"You have that contemplative look. What is it, Evelyn?" His voice was deep with concern, and a wary look had entered his piercing eyes.

"I was wondering if you've ever made love under the stars," she blurted. The comment astonished them both. She couldn't believe the words came out of her mouth, and he looked like someone had punched him in the ballsack. "Forget I said anything," she mumbled as she rolled away.

He halted her before her feet hit the ground. "Tiff was the only woman I've been with."

Evelyn almost fell off the stone altar. "What?"

"You know our history; we met when we were in high school. As for after…" He flopped his head back on the pillow of his arm and shrugged with one shoulder. "It isn't as if I haven't been in the mood to have sex, but I honestly didn't have the time or the opportunity. Because of my position at the FBI, I also have to be extremely careful in who I choose to bring home with me."

"Dude."

He snorted a laugh. "Pathetic, huh?"

"Not in the least. I guess I never dreamed I'd be the more experienced of the two of us."

"You forget I've known you forever, Evelyn. Your dating history wasn't plentiful, and it was downright painful in its—"

"Dude!" She shoved him. "I'm so not discussing this with you."

His wide grin lit up the night and brought back the urgent need to kiss him.

"Let's get back to Alastair's before he sends the cavalry for us." Looking at Simon was difficult and brought with it a very real fear she'd beg him to rock her world right then and there, so she avoided his watchful gaze.

"What about you?"

"Excuse me?" she squeaked and whipped her head back around to stare at him.

"Have you ever made love under the stars?"

His tone dipped into dangerous. Something shifted in his expression, and all of his attention was focused on her. There was a stillness to him as if he were waiting for the right moment to strike. But Evelyn couldn't, for the life of her, figure out where the sudden fierceness came from.

She grimaced. "I wouldn't call it making love. Groping and an unsatisfying quickie best describe it. The guy I was dating was a two-pump chump."

Simon's laughter rang out and echoed around them. The sound was so joyful, Evelyn was awed by this unguarded side of him. Always, he'd kept himself in check, reserved. And yes, they'd been friends. Including Tiffany and whomever Evelyn had been dating at the time, they'd made up a foursome for dinners or random work functions. But Evelyn and Tiff had maintained the closer friendship. At least, that had been the case up until the time she'd gotten sick and Simon had needed a friend to talk to. Oddly, it was only when his wife's condition was declared terminal that he'd begun confiding in Evelyn like a true friend would.

It took a second for her to register the laughter had left him and he was once again staring at her with a barely leashed emotion that was hard to define.

Her gaze sought the thing she desired most—his mouth. And when his lips parted, she almost whimpered her need. Time seemed suspended as he rolled to a sitting position and tugged her to kneel between his sprawled-out thighs. It gave her a slight height advantage, and the moonlight showed his handsome visage to advantage. The raw desire on his face couldn't be mistaken for anything else.

He pulled his eyes from where they'd been locked with hers and watched his own hand as he placed it over her heart. His palm was warm through the material of her jersey shirt. In a strange way, it felt as if he were branding her.

Ever so slowly, he trailed his palm upward, and his fingers tickled her skin as they skimmed the hollows of her throat. As soon as they were curled around her neck, he gently drew her forward. When their lips were a hairsbreadth away, he whispered her name.

Evelyn closed the last little distance between them and pressed her mouth to his. His tongue swept across her lower lip, and she parted for him. In the span of a heartbeat, he was kissing her like she'd never been kissed before. As if she were necessary. As if without her, he'd cease to exist. She could feel his desperation to claim her, and she silently rejoiced as she straddled his lap.

"Let's make love under the stars, Evelyn."

His husky request sent a delighted shiver through her. Words escaped her, and all she could do was nod her agreement.

Finesse deserted them, and they fell on each other with wild abandon. Buttons went flying, and jeans were shucked. They were two love-starved individuals who had found their other half. His touch sent her soaring, and when he thrust into her for the first time, she sighed her contentment. To feel him inside her, filling, stretching, *completing* her, was pure bliss.

Her fingers dug into the contoured muscles of his ass, and she urged him on with frantic cries of "more" as she pulled him closer and crushed her pelvis to his. His name became a chant, a plea, as the slap of flesh on flesh increased in tempo.

As she flew over the precipice toward her orgasm, she gripped his head and drew him down to her. "Come with me, Simon Says," she ordered.

And he did.

Joy filled her as he shouted her name, and her magic thrummed through her body, creating a golden glow around them.

"That's a bit freaky," he managed between pants. "But I kind of like it."

His harsh breathing made her grin. *She'd* done that. She'd given him that satisfaction.

Simon pressed his forehead to hers as he settled his sweat-slick torso against hers. "I like to feel you fully against me, but let me know if I'm too heavy."

Laughing, she hooked her legs around his waist and hugged him so tightly her breasts ached from the pressure. "You could never be too heavy. I would stay this way forever if I could."

"It's a fantasy of mine," he said in an embarrassed voice.

"What is? Lying together like this?" She tried not to preen with the knowledge he'd fantasized about her.

"Yes. Of making love to you and staying joined until I could take you again. Stopping only long enough to eat or shower. Perhaps take a cat nap until we woke and started all over."

"Why, Simon Says, I love the way you think," she drawled with a light laugh.

"Shut up and kiss me," he growled playfully.

She gave him a teasing grin. "You have to say it properly."

"Simon Says, shut up and kiss me, Evelyn Thorne, then prepare for round two."

CHAPTER 16

They walked back to the house, hand in hand. Simon loved the feel of her cool palm cradled within his. Too much. He'd royally fucked up when he made love to her in the clearing. She'd expect more, and he couldn't give it. And yet, he couldn't find the words to tell her as much.

"You're thinking too hard, Simon Says," she said with a wry tone.

A glance showed her sporting a sad half-smile.

The words he wanted to say locked in his throat.

"It's okay." She squeezed his hand. "I understand why we can't have a lasting relationship."

His heart contracted along with her fingers. "I want one. With you."

"And I want one. With you." She settled her head on his shoulder as they strolled on.

"After we take down Pete, maybe we can appeal to The Authority." The uncertainty in his own voice made him wince.

"And if they deny our appeal, maybe we can do something bizarre like all those classic movies." She turned to face him and skipped backwards down the path. "We'll meet once a year at the top of the

Empire State Building and have a weekend of love. Or book a cruise to have one joyous week together, every six months or so."

Simon adored this side of Evelyn. Her fun, carefree nature contrasted with her work persona, but this was the version of her he preferred. "What do we do for the remaining part of the year?"

"Video chats, phone sex, sexting, or virtual sex. The sky is the limit."

He laughed; he couldn't help himself. "Virtual sex? Like putting on those ridiculous goggles and humping air?"

"Admittedly, I haven't worked that one through yet. But we'll figure it out."

Using their connected hands, he pulled her to a stop and straight into his arms for a searing kiss. "We'll have to figure it out soon. Now that I've had a taste, I'm reluctant to go back to an empty home."

As she smoothed the hair back from his brow, she gave him a look filled with such love, his knees grew weak and his heart began to hammer painfully in his chest. No words were needed between them. They were definitely on the same page.

Once more, she fell into step beside him. As one, they stopped and stared at the looming mansion of Alastair Thorne.

"What does he do for a living?"

Evelyn laughed. "Why? You think he's into nefarious dealings?"

"I don't care if he is. I'm simply curious."

"He used to be the CEO of Thorne Industries before he turned it over to his son, Nash. Now, he dabbles in stocks and a few minor business ventures. I'm certain he has a Midas touch." She shrugged. "His business acumen is probably assisted by his empath ability. He can read people like no one else, and I'm sure it helps him determine who the shysters are."

"I like him."

"And he likes you, or you wouldn't be within a hundred yards of me. You certainly wouldn't have been invited to his home. He rarely reveals the location for safety purposes."

Simon gave her a sharp look. "He has a lot of enemies?"

"Enough. Or he used to. He's feared in the witch community, and rightfully so. Alastair is very no-nonsense and will destroy anyone who comes after his family."

Her smile was warm as she talked about her cousin, and Simon knew a moment of envy, but he shoved it away. It didn't matter that he only had an absentee brother for family. He had his work, and in the future, he'd find a way to have Evelyn on a permanent basis that wouldn't end her life.

"You're always sad when you think about your family, Simon Says," she said softly. "The Thornes are yours now, too."

"Doubtful. Especially when they learn I'm cursed and likely to cause your untimely death."

"Nope. They'll embrace you and help us figure out a cure. You'll see."

Her assurance gave him hope.

"Let's go get some sleep, Simon. Tomorrow will take care of itself."

EVELYN HATED SIMON'S UNCERTAINTY, BUT SHE'D NEVER VOICE IT. THE worry he was feeling could be seen in his haunted eyes, and she wished she could ease his pain. But she couldn't. Grief was a funny thing. One day, a person was mindlessly going about their business, with no hint of sadness, and then it struck. The death of a loved one could feel as real at that moment as it had on the day of their passing. It had the potential to ruin an entire day, week, or month if one allowed themselves to dwell. But also, grief could be fleeting, and a person could be back to normal within an hour or so.

She'd experienced it about family members and Tiffany.

Simon had to feel the effects of Tiff's passing even more.

"The fact we love each other isn't a betrayal of Tiffany, you know." It needed to be said. Her timing might be faulty, but she wasn't one for letting things fester.

"I know." His tone was sure, but his eyes told a different tale.

"Simon." She touched his cheek and didn't speak until he met her gaze. "It isn't a betrayal. She wanted you to find love again, remember? She was trying to match us the moment she heard the news her condition was terminal."

"I didn't love you then. Not in that way."

"I know. And I refused to allow those feelings to take hold back then either. We were two friends and work colleagues. Nothing more. Nothing less."

"Then why do I feel like a shit? Like I *am* betraying her?"

Evelyn tilted her head slightly to study him. His guilt and sorrow were present and building steam. "I don't think you do, Simon Says. Not about us. I think it has to do with finding out you are a latent Death Dealer. That whatever residual power you have spilled over, and that it could again."

"I couldn't live with myself if you died because of me, Evelyn. I just couldn't," he said raggedly.

Alastair's voice came from the shadows. "And perhaps your grief and guilt stem from surviving Tiffany's loss only to love again. For your life not ending when hers did."

Not surprised by the assessment, Evelyn silently agreed as she watched the play of emotions on Simon's face: irritation, anger, and finally, resignation.

"Perhaps," Simon conceded.

"Evelyn, Aurora prepared the blue room for you. If you would run along, I'd like to speak to your young man."

"I don't believe in shotgun weddings, cuz," she warned. "And I'm only going because I'm tired and need sleep. Don't harass Simon."

"As if I ever would." Alastair sniffed in faux indignation and straightened his cuffs. "Begone, you willful child."

She laughed and kissed her cousin's cheek, then turned to Simon. "He's not as scary as he seems. You're welcome to join me when you're finished."

"Actually, I'd prefer he didn't until we figure out how to neutralize his effect on your health," Alastair said with a seriousness she hated.

"I'm afraid you're about to close the barn door after the horse is gone, Al." She crinkled her nose and shrugged. "We consummated our relationship in the clearing."

He stilled. "What did you say?"

"We did the nasty a few times. And no, I'm not sorry."

"*In the clearing?* Where precisely in the clearing?" Alastair's tone was as severe as she'd ever heard, and her heart began to pound so hard she feared it would come out through her shirt.

She tossed an alarmed look Simon's way, only to find him red-faced and gaping like a landed fish. Her funny bone was tickled, and she did her damnedest not to release an inappropriate laugh.

Alastair commanded her attention. "Tell me it wasn't on the altar, Evelyn. Tell me you weren't so foolish."

Taking umbrage, she placed her hands on her hips. "I'm never foolish or careless, Alastair. Why don't you tell me what this is about?"

His damned empathic ability gave her away, though, and his expression said there would be hell to pay. Very soon, if she wasn't mistaken.

CHAPTER 17

"That land—specifically the stone circle—is sacred. If either of you had any magical knowledge between you, you'd understand you can't simply do the *'nasty'* there a couple of times without consequence."

Alastair's anger was a living thing, and it lashed them like a whip. Simon understood genuine fear of a magical being for the first time in his life.

"Rein it in, Alastair," Evelyn warned. "You'll hurt someone if you don't."

"Please explain, Mr. Thorne," Simon requested.

Alastair inhaled and exhaled a few long, slow breaths as if he were making a concerted effort to shrug off his irritation and get his emotions in hand. "As Evelyn so eloquently stated, you consummated your relationship. If you have sexual relations in a sacred place, you're pledging yourself to one another. The gods and goddesses view it as binding."

Evelyn's entire countenance drained of color. "No one ever told me about that little humping-on-holy-ground caveat."

"What does it mean to be bound to one another?" Simon asked as he tried to ignore how much her horror hurt his feelings. He didn't get why making love in a clearing was a bad thing or why it would matter to deities where they were when they did the deed. "Are we talking a supernatural marriage here or what?"

"Or what," Alastair confirmed with a grim expression. "Come. Let's have a drink, and I'll explain what I know." He led them into his study, gestured for them to sit, then poured them each their preferred drink; wine for Evelyn and scotch for Simon and himself.

Alastair perched on the edge of his desk and stared into the amber contents of his drink for a long moment before taking an appreciative sip. With a sigh, he placed his tumbler down beside him, then said, "Unless I'm dreadfully wrong, you've had a joining of the souls, and Evelyn is in grave danger due to spiritual exposure to a Death Dealer."

The blood drained from Simon's head, and dizziness assailed him. Evelyn's sickly expression had to match what he was sure was his own. "We saw a golden glow… that was the joining of souls, wasn't it?"

"I'm afraid so, son."

Evelyn rallied quicker than Simon expected, considering her life was on the line. "I'm sure many people have had sex there, Al, all without binding themselves. What makes us different?"

"Love. Timing. And unless I miss my guess, the altar."

She locked gazes with Simon, and they both recognized they'd screwed the pooch, so to speak. If he wasn't terribly concerned, he'd have been overjoyed. As it was, he needed to know the facts to mitigate the damage done. He tore his gaze from hers and focused on Alastair. "The combining of souls, how does that hurt her if she isn't around me?"

"In the exchange, your magic mingles together. Each of you consumes a small measure of the other's power. Not enough to use it to advantage, though," Alastair explained. "But by taking in yours, she's opened herself up to a greater magic than she can possibly handle."

"How can this be undone?" Simon demanded.

"Spring or Isis would be my best guess."

Evelyn rubbed the spot between her brows, and Simon noticed some of the color had returned to her cheeks.

"Tell me, Alastair, when couples get married in the clearing, do they exchange power like Simon and I did?"

"It depends on the couple and the magic they possess. A standard marriage ceremony between two witches is usually officiated by one of the Witches' Council members and takes place on sacred ground. But most couples don't consummate their marriage there. *Most* have been warned against it."

"Because sharing of powers can be dangerous," Simon concluded.

"If the conditions, such as yours, are right, then yes." Alastair sipped his drink and stared out the window toward the glen where they'd been. "This particular land holds more ancient magic than most. There are standing stones underground, and they can amplify… *things*."

Evelyn downed the last of her wine and set the glass on the side table. "Well, there is nothing to be done about it tonight. I suppose we should get some sleep and regroup in the morning. After I wake up, I'll call Spring and see what she knows."

Simon smiled as he squeezed Evelyn's hand. "Ever practical."

"And ever a grump if I don't get sleep," she retorted with a slight scowl. "Come on. If we are going to hell in a handbasket for our mistake, then we should at least enjoy the trip."

"That's not conducive to sleep," he felt compelled to point out.

"Maybe not, but what the hell?"

Simon stood and helped her to her feet. With a tender kiss and a light nudge, he said, "Go on. I'll follow shortly."

"Don't be long, Simon Says."

"I wouldn't dream of it."

After Evelyn exited the study, Simon faced Alastair. "How bad is it?"

"You're a Death Dealer, son. You tell me."

He snorted and took a fortifying sip of scotch, then said, "The likelihood is that you know more about who and what I am than I ever will, Mr. Thorne."

Alastair acknowledged his comment with a half-smile and a nod. From his desk, he picked up a thick, bound book. He handed it off to

Simon. "Here's a little light reading for you. Your brother recommended you do so as soon as possible. He wanted me to tell you he'll be available whenever you want to talk."

"Did he go home?"

"No. He's staying in the guest house just beyond the garden." Alastair's expression turned grave. "I believe he's self-isolating because of his profession. It's a lonely existence."

"You sound as if you speak from experience."

"I do. I wouldn't wish it for you or your brother."

"You're married now. What changed?" Simon asked.

"Rorie woke up."

Metaphorically or in reality, he didn't know, and although Alastair Thorne seemed to be in a chatty mood, Simon was somewhat hesitant to ask him.

"Did your team learn anything from Evelyn's intruder?"

"No. As she stated earlier, he didn't know anything. The head of my security, Martin, is working on it as we speak. Ryker gained permission from one of the Council members to search the archives for Pete Wilson and known associates. I, however, have a feeling he won't discover anything relevant." Alastair finished off his scotch and placed the tumbler next to Evelyn's used wine glass. Both disappeared in an instant.

"What the fuck?" Simon blinked twice and refocused, but the glasses were gone.

Alastair laughed and clapped him on the shoulder. "I have a very obsessive-compulsive butler. I'll introduce you to Alfred tomorrow."

CHAPTER 18

After Alastair showed him to the bedroom he'd been assigned, Simon bid him good night. He'd been informed Evelyn's room was to the left of his, but he was reluctant to join her after what he'd learned. Flipping open the tome in his hand, he began to read.

He became fully engrossed in the information given to him, unaware of the passing time. The soft tap on his door caught his attention, and he opened it to find a sleepy-looking Evelyn on the other side.

"Hey, Simon Says."

"Hey."

Every instinct screamed at him to invite her in, but he blocked the entrance to his room.

Confusion and hurt filled her face, but just as quickly, it disappeared, leaving her with a carefully neutral expression. "I just wanted to make sure you were okay after your conversation with Alastair." She gave him a tight smile. "Good night."

As she turned to go, Simon touched her shoulder. "Evelyn."

She stopped but didn't face him.

"I…" What could he say? That he'd been studying up on the type of monster he had the potential to be? That, in reading, he confirmed he'd unknowingly been responsible for his wife's death? That, in all likelihood, he'd be responsible for Evelyn's now that they shared a spiritual bond? In the end, all he said was "Good night."

She nodded once and left him with his demons.

Her closed door stared at him accusingly, and Simon desperately wanted to explain. Eventually he would, but there wasn't much point in hashing things out in the small hours of the morning when there was a criminal on the loose who wanted to serve up Simon as a patsy. Or see him dead.

He walked to the nightstand and picked up his smartphone. Evelyn wasn't wrong when she said the carefully planned set-up against him needed to be resolved with magic. But it might be better if he utilized his family's rather than hers. He shot off a text to his brother, then waited. If Trevor was awake, they'd meet and formulate a plan.

Ten minutes later, his brother was seated across from him in one of the guest-room armchairs.

"You look tired, Trev."

"More world-weary than anything. This job is getting old."

Simon nodded. An occupation as an angel of death would definitely take its toll. "But you also have the ability to give life, right?"

Trevor opened his mouth to respond, closed it into a grim line, then finally replied, "When allowed by the Authority, yes."

"It all comes down to the Authority, doesn't it?" Simon knocked the book hard with his knuckles. "Those damned Fates like to control everything."

"They certainly don't like it when their timeline is altered."

"But there are Travelers. They alter things at whim."

"The Fates step in when a Traveler gets out of hand. Besides, Travelers are rare. There are only two that I'm aware of."

"We both met one today. Who is the other?"

"Alexander Castor. He recently popped up on the Authority's radar and is the one to watch. Apparently, he faked his own death, and he has an uncanny ability to avoid detection."

Simon didn't like what he was learning and experienced a sense of unease. "The Authority sounds cultish and militant."

"I can see why you'd think that," Trev said with a grimace. "And maybe they can be. Mostly they allow the Witches' Council to police the magical community. But when the Council fails, we step in."

"If Dad is supposedly dead, then why continue to bind my powers?" Simon had learned a little about the Authority through the book his brother provided, along with the answers he'd given. The pressing need to discover more about their father became the most prominent. "I can't believe he wouldn't contact us."

"That's the question of the hour. I've been reaching out to contacts for most of the evening, and Dad's a ghost. No one has seen him."

"No one but Alastair," Simon replied sourly. "You honestly didn't know?"

Irritation laced with anger flashed on Trevor's face. "No. I already told you as much. But I'm damned sure going to find him and demand answers."

"We'll find him together. I need to get a handle on this cursed ability of ours. I want to know why the Authority saw fit to bind my powers and how we undo it. I'll have no life if I don't."

"You'll have no life if you do."

"Trev—"

His brother held up a hand to forestall any objection. "We won't get into this, but promise you'll leave that poor woman in peace. Neither of us needs Alastair Thorne on our ass if something happens to her." Something in Simon's expression must've revealed the truth because Trevor groaned. "You've got to be fucking kidding me, Si. What did you do?"

"I may have inadvertently bound our souls tonight."

"Christ!"

"Yeah, my thoughts exactly," Simon replied heavily. "I don't know what to do."

"Try to keep your distance, but also stay in touch. The moment she gets a sniffle, you call me, and I'll do what I can to reverse the damage."

"I thought you said you can't heal without the Authority's

approval?"

"Fuck them. This is family. Also, I doubt they would withhold it. No one, the Fates included, wants to be on Alastair's bad side. The Goddess Isis has his back, and he's cousin to the Aether."

"Would I be showing my ignorance by asking about the Aether?" Simon asked with a half-smile.

Trevor closed his eyes and groaned. "Seriously?"

"I didn't get to that part of the book."

"Right. The damned thing should start with him." Trevor conjured a beer, slouched down in the chair, and crossed his long legs at the ankles. "Do you want one? This might be a lengthy explanation." When Simon shook his head, his brother took a pull of his drink. "Damian Dethridge—"

Simon stopped him with a bark of laughter. "Really? Damian Dethridge is his name? He sounds like a hero in a romance novel. Like maybe he should have our ability. Damian Dethridge—Death Dealer!"

"Laugh it up, you tool. He not only has *our* ability, he has *everyone's* ability."

Simon was dumbfounded. "How so?"

"The Aether is the balance between good and evil. He needs to possess every power known to man in order to keep that balance." Admiration shone from Trevor's eyes. "Even the gods and goddesses fear him. He took on the Enchantress *and* the Darkness and won."

"I don't know what any of that means," Simon admitted.

"Doesn't matter. Bottom line: the Aether is a badass and no one fucks with him if they want to live to tell the tale."

"I'll make a note of it," Simon said dryly. Another thought occurred to him, one that gave him hope. "If Dethridge is so powerful, can he heal Evelyn if she needs it?"

Trevor stopped with the beer halfway to his lips. "That's a good point. I'd say yes, but we could check with Alastair to be sure." He was about to resume drinking when his expression changed to one of wonder. "I bet he could seal the cracks in your power. Or take it away completely."

"Really?" Simon's heart began to pound with excitement. He lived his entire life without magic, and he'd only seen the negative side of what his could do. If there was someone who could remove his ability for good and let him live a normal life with Evelyn, he'd sign up immediately.

"I don't know why Alastair didn't think of it first."

"I'm sure he did."

Trevor's brows shot up.

"Think about it, Trev. I get the impression magical knowledge is important to Alastair. He gets highly irate when he doesn't feel that knowledge is utilized or passed on the way it should. It makes me think he believes in free will." Simon grabbed the dangling beer from his brother's hand, took a sip, and handed it back. "If we know what we are capable of, we can make our own decisions and clean up our own messes. Everyone is less dependent on him, which leaves him free to live his life as the black sheep of the magical community—just the way he likes it."

Trevor nodded slowly. "You may be right. By providing us with the information, we can discover what we need and work together to come up with a handy solution to our problem." He shrugged. "Sounds exactly like Alastair."

"I don't know him at all, other than through stories Evelyn has told, but yeah, that's what I think, too."

"Well, I suppose our next step would be talking to Damian Dethridge." His brother rose to his feet and arched his back. "But I do need a few hours of sleep."

"Wilson is first. Evelyn will be safe enough under Alastair's watchful eye between now and when you and I find that dickhead, Pete. I need to remove the target from her back before I can think about a relationship."

"I'll try scrying in the morning. When I find him, I'll make him write and sign a confession, clearing your name. Trust me, he'll meet his maker," Trevor promised with a fervent gleam. "He chose the wrong man to pin his crimes on."

CHAPTER 19

*E*velyn swiped a hand over the mirror to remove the evidence of her spying, and faced Alastair. "You're a sneaky bastard, cuz."

His lips twitched, and his sapphire eyes sparkled with delight. "Am I? Where is your proof?"

"Did you miss what I just saw?"

"Not a single word."

"Like I said, sneaky," she said with a light laugh. "Thank you."

He shrugged one shoulder, stood, and took the empty wine glass from her hand. "Go get sleep. I have Martin and Ryker investigating Pete. As soon as I know something, I'll wake you."

"Will Damian remove the last of Simon's power, do you think? He doesn't want it." Evelyn didn't dare hope. Spending what remained of her life with Simon was important to her, but she'd rather not experience a horrible death like Tiffany's.

"He will if I ask him, but not without double-checking to see if the Authority or the Council have a hidden agenda. We'll have to be patient and wait for him to report back, but I'm confident you'll be safe enough as long as Damian is available to remove the negative side effects Simon has on you."

"That sounds dire. Is there a risk of Damian not being around?"

"He's two-hundred-years old, and you never know what life will bring. As your young man's brother stated, Damian fought both the Enchantress and the Darkness. The last was touch and go for the group of us." Alastair shrugged. "My main takeaway from all the trials I've survived is this: you have to live your best life by any means possible." He tilted her chin up and met her gaze without blinking. "Don't let anything stand in your way, child. Not Pete, not the Authority, and certainly not this little glitch of Simon's. We'll find a work-around for it. Always grab the bull by the horns and ride it for all you're worth."

His passionate little speech made her strangely emotional. Alastair had faced challenge after challenge with a bold determination the likes she'd never seen before or since. He'd never given up when his soulmate, Aurora, had gone into stasis and remained in the coma-like state for nearly two decades. Armed with nothing more than an enviable love, he sought her out in the Otherworld, and he eventually made a pact with Isis. He'd been prepared to sacrifice himself and whatever else was necessary to bring Aurora back from the dead. And he'd managed it, despite all odds. Giving in to the urge to hug him, Evelyn wrapped her arms around his waist and rested her cheek on his chest.

"I will," she promised, as she silently told herself she would be just like him. She'd be the type of person who would traverse to the other side to bring Simon back to her if she had to.

His arms came around her, and he held her tightly until her sudden melancholy fled. "There is no greater prize on earth than that of true love, child."

"I know. You're an inspiration to us all."

He drew back and smiled down at her. "Am I?" At her nod, he tapped her nose. "Good to know I have some usefulness."

"Pfft. You're a legend."

Before he could respond, a cool, cultured voice interrupted. "Is that what they are writing on the walls of the women's loo?"

Evelyn wouldn't have said it was possible for Alastair to physically express such strong emotion, but the second his gaze touched on his mate, his face lit up and the love shining from his eyes was breathtaking in its beauty.

"Rorie."

Aurora's love for him was just as strong. "Darling. I wondered what was keeping you, and here I find you conspiring with Evelyn. I'm certain you're up to no good." Even in a bathrobe with her pixie-cut black hair highlighted with cobalt-blue, she had an air of royalty about her. Her dark brows lifted in challenge. "Am I wrong?"

With a grin of appreciation, Alastair wrapped an arm around Aurora's waist and pulled her close. "Never. And even if you were, I'd be a fool to correct you."

Musical laughter flowed from her, and the sound was enchanting. "Come to bed, darling. There's something that needs your immediate attention."

The devilish sparkle in Aurora's sky-blue eyes said exactly what that something was, and it made Evelyn feel like a voyeur. "I'll head back to my room and leave you to it," she said. "Thank you for letting me steal him for a bit, Rorie."

All teasing left Aurora. "Did you get everything resolved?"

"Not yet, but we're almost there," Alastair assured her.

"Good. Tomorrow we'll all get to work on your behalf, Evelyn," Aurora said. "Pete Wilson, that tosser, will be apprehended before the week is out. Then you and Simon will have your happily ever after."

Evelyn's desire to question how Aurora knew all that she did was strong, but she held her tongue and thanked them both. She didn't want to bust her hostess for spying when she'd been doing the same thing a few minutes before.

The sparkle of laughter lurking in Alastair's eyes said he caught the slip, too. "You shouldn't scry, love. No good can come of it."

"Pot meet kettle. You're the one who turned me to a life of crime, darling."

He chuckled and didn't refute her claim. "Say good night to Evelyn, Rorie. I'm taking you back to bed."

The couple never spared Evelyn a glance as Aurora trilled a farewell. They were gone in a blink.

And wasn't that the beauty of teleporting? It took less than a heartbeat to return to the bedroom, strip down, and begin the sexual games.

Evelyn grinned as she teleported to her own room. *Ah, if only Simon had decided to join her.*

CHAPTER 20

Five hours later, Evelyn knocked on Simon's door, and she caught her breath when it swung open. Simon, sleep rumpled in a pair of lounge pants and form-fitting t-shirt, looked good enough to eat. Maybe it was the way the white sleeves were tightly stretched over his muscled biceps and rounded shoulders, or perhaps it was the day-old stubble darkening his jawline, but he appeared vastly different than the put-together man in a suit she usually saw. Only when Tiffany was in the last stages of her illness had he appeared unkempt, and Evelyn's thoughts during that time were as far away from sexual as they could get.

"You shouldn't stare at me like that, Evelyn." His voice was pitched low and held a grittiness associated with little sleep. She'd heard it often enough when they'd worked overtime on a case.

She couldn't help but smile. "Will it make you go all caveman and drag me into your lair? If so, I'm all for it."

He laughed, and her heart felt lighter. She'd been worried he'd decided to reject her on a more permanent basis, even after what she'd learned by scrying last night.

"Alastair will have a large spread in the dining room. I believe

Alfred likes to cater to the masses when my cousin is in planning mode."

"Planning mode?"

"It's sort of what we call it when he rallies the troops to fight the current big baddie. There will be plate-size cinnamon rolls and every delectable fruit imaginable. Perfectly scrambled eggs and fresh-baked croissants."

Simon surprised a squeak from her when he pulled her into a tight hug. "Marry me so I can become a Thorne, please."

"That's the only reason you'd marry me?" She smiled as she rubbed her nose in the crease of his neck, inhaling his unique woodsy scent. Whatever pheromones he put off turned her knees to jelly and caused her heart to beat faster. At the same time, it soothed her and made her happy. "Typically, a woman marries into a man's family and takes his name. Not the other way around."

"I'm a modern man. I don't mind being known as Simon Thorne." His hands trailed down to cup her ass, causing her to tilt her hips and press more fully against him. "It sounds a bit badass, and no one will care to mess with me."

"Mmm, I agree it *is* pretty badass. Though, I hate to break it to you; the Thorne name will bring enemies out of the woodwork." Drawing her upper body back just enough to see his face, she smiled. "However, if that was a legitimate proposal, I accept. We might as well make it legal now that we're bound by the deities."

With a grimace and a quick kiss of her forehead, Simon released her. "I have an action plan, and if it turns out like I hope, then you can consider my proposal legitimate. If not…" He shrugged, and a miserable expression crossed his face. "Well, I don't know where to go from there."

"I wouldn't worry about it, Simon Says. These things have a way of working out." This one would. She'd make sure of it, even if she had to confront the Authority herself. "Do you want to wait for your morning wood to go the rest of the way down, or should we take care of that before breakfast?"

He groaned and turned his back to her, but not before she saw his dick twitch in response to her suggestion.

"You're killing me, Evelyn. You know that, right?"

"I don't know why you have to protest like a Victorian debutante, but okay." She patted his ass and stepped into the hallway. "I'll meet you in the dining room, m'lady."

"You have a mouth on you, Thorne."

"I offered to put it to good use." A wicked laugh escaped her when she witnessed his reaction to her comment. "You've known me for twenty-plus years, Simon Says. Why would that surprise you?"

"It wasn't that. It was the image of—" he shook his head "—forget it. Get going so I can grab a five-minute shower and kill this hard-on."

With narrowed eyes and a longing in her soul, she said, "Not fair to tease me."

This time, it was his laugh that was deliciously wicked. "You'll know when I'm teasing you, Evelyn Thorne, and you'll beg me to end it."

Two seconds away from begging anyway, she gave a careless shrug. "Promises, promises. See you in the dining room." She paused in turning away. "Do you know how to get there? I can always wait next door until you're ready."

"Wasn't it right down the hall from Alastair's study?"

"Yep." Because she couldn't resist one last caress of his body with her eyes, she looked her fill and smiled at what she saw. "Later, Simon Says."

"Brat," he hollered at her retreating back.

On her way downstairs, she encountered Trevor.

"Good morning," she said brightly. It wouldn't hurt to be on good terms with Simon's family. It would be nice to have his brother visit if she were to someday tie the knot with Simon for real.

The seriousness on Trevor's face bothered her. Sure, the situation wasn't ideal, but for the moment they were well protected and out of Pete's reach. "Are you okay, Mr. Blane?"

"Yeah," he said with a tired sigh. "Peachy."

"Want to talk about it?"

"I should probably have this conversation with Simon first."

"Have you eaten breakfast yet, Mr. Blane?"

"Please call me Trevor or Trev. I hate formality when it comes to friends."

Evelyn tilted her head to study his interesting face. He struck her as more GQ than Simon, but they both had a natural air of command about them. In a bygone era, they'd have been lords of some manor house or estate somewhere. Thanks to endless FBI training and their strict fitness requirements for his specific division, Simon was more powerfully built, but Trevor could probably hold his own in a fight.

"Thank you for considering me a friend, Trevor. Now come—" she tucked her arm through his "—let's go have a cup of coffee and chat while Simon is in the shower. You can tell me what's bothering you."

He looked beyond her toward his brother's room then returned his gaze to her. "Lead on."

"I know you intended to look into your father's whereabouts. What did you discover?"

"A friend working for the Authority assured me dear old Dad is alive and well." The grimness in his tone didn't disguise the hurt.

"I'm sorry."

Trevor stopped walking to give her an incredulous look. "That's he's alive?"

"No. Because he was an absentee father and never made an effort to contact either of you. Neither you nor Simon deserved it. I believed him to be a good person based on Simon's recollections of him."

With a brisk nod, he led her down the stairs. "I never expected much from him. He'd told me early on what we were and made me promise to keep it from Simon. My training was strict and brutal," he confessed.

"Let me guess. All those years Simon thought you were happily away at school; you were going through the rigors of the Authority's program on how to be a good little Death Dealer?"

"Got it in one."

"No wonder you're a stuffed shirt."

He snorted an incredulous laugh. "Excuse me?"

"Don't take this the wrong way, but you strike me as aloof. Would I be wrong to say you don't let many people close?"

His smile, when it came, was breathtaking in its beauty. His entire face softened and gained a boyishness, making him look years younger. "You're an excellent profiler, and you wouldn't be wrong, Ms. Thorne."

"Evelyn," she corrected.

"Will Simon be all right when we confirm our father is alive, do you think?"

Trevor's uncertainty surprised her. Yes, she'd known he didn't come around often, if at all, but she would've bet money he had kept tabs on Simon's life. "I imagine he'll feel as you do: hurt and angry, with a burning desire for answers," she finally said. "But I promise, he'll be okay."

"You're a better fit for him than Tiffany ever was," Trevor said in a low voice, as if afraid to be overheard. "He would never listen to anything critical about her, but she wasn't the saint he believed her to be."

A sudden shiver swept through Evelyn, accompanied by a chilling thought. Pulling away, she stared up at him; her shocking suspicion caused her to stumble over the words. "You didn't... um, you..."

"No. I didn't hasten her death. I promise." He gave her a tight smile. "I'm sad you had to ask."

"I'm sorry. In fairness, I don't know you, Trevor, and I imagine based on your occupation, you're forced to cross the line."

"True enough, and no offense taken." He placed a hand on her lower back, and a pulsing heat ran the length of her spine.

She jumped. "What was that?"

A grin tugged at his lips. "Call it a booster shot for longevity."

"To counter any health-stealing magic that might come my way due to my association with your brother?"

"Exactly."

Gratitude for his small rebellion filled her heart, and Evelyn rose on the tips of her toes to kiss his cheek. "Thank you. I won't tell a soul, and hopefully, the Authority will never find out."

"If they do, they do. You're Simon's true family now. It comes with perks."

She rested her head on his shoulder as they walked the rest of the way to the dining room in silence. Right before they reached the sideboard buffet, she stopped him with a hand on his arm. "If you should ever need anything, all you need to do is ask. The Thornes will have your back. You have my word."

His warm smile reached his eyes as he patted her hand. "Thanks. I'll remember to use that line if I get called before the Fates on account of my actions."

CHAPTER 21

Simon paused in the doorway of the dining room, a little overwhelmed by the size of the extended Thorne family. He met his brother's wry gaze from across the distance, and it registered that Trevor was feeling much the same way.

Evelyn's shiny blonde head was visible beyond Quentin's shoulder as the man leaned in to speak to a woman on his left, with thick chestnut-colored hair. Ever so carefully, he removed a small toddler from the woman's arms, blew a raspberry on the girl's cheek, and tucked her on his lap.

As Simon approached, he heard Quentin imitate a prop plane as he teased the little tyke with a spoonful of purple food.

"Plums," Evelyn said from her spot across the table. "It's Frankie's favorite meal."

Abruptly, young Frankie turned her wide eyes on Simon. For two long heartbeats, she watched him curiously, and once she reached some internal decision, she held out her arms for him to lift her.

He had to laugh at the astonishment on the faces around him as Quentin handed his child off to him. "Babies love me. What can I say?"

"And dogs," Trevor added. "When we were kids, packs of dogs

would follow him home. If anyone in the neighborhood was missing a pet, they came to our house first."

"They literally followed him home?" the woman Simon assumed was Quentin's wife asked. She turned her curious gaze his way and gave him an assessing look. "I can see why," she murmured loud enough for those closest to her to hear.

Evelyn laughed heartily as Quentin poked his wife in the ribs.

"What? I call it like I see it," the woman stated matter-of-factly.

Simon liked her instantly. He held out his hand. "Simon Blane."

"Holly Buchanan, nee Thorne. Alastair's my father," she said by way of introduction.

"Ah, you're the 'prickly pear' Quentin needed to hide from when he offered to run away with Evelyn." Simon dodged sideways in case the guy decided to strike. He didn't need to. Apparently, Quentin knew how to charm his wife.

"Don't listen to him, Hol. You know I'd never leave you and my beloved Frankie, traitor that she is."

Ignoring him, Holly leaned forward to tell Evelyn, "You can have him if you want. His feet stink, and he farts in bed."

Quentin laughed and drew Holly onto his lap for a long, drawn-out kiss that had a few of the table's occupants clearing their throats at the passionate PDA. A clear reminder from the grown-ups that others were present, most especially children.

Of course, he ignored them.

When he ended the kiss, Holly's cheeks were red as berries, and her eyes glowed with adoration. "Now take it back, Hol," Quentin urged in a cajoling voice.

She dutifully said, "His feet don't stink." And when her husband raised his brows, she added, "And he only farts in bed after he's had chili dogs."

Again, Quentin laughed, shaking his head as he picked up a croissant and tore a piece off. Holly remained securely on his lap with one arm around his neck as he lovingly fed her little bites of the bread.

"Either of you want your kid back?" Simon asked, completely charmed by the three of them.

Frankie shook her head and patted his cheeks. "Pums!"

Left with no choice, Simon sat down and took the proffered bowl and spoon from Quentin. "Fine, but I don't make airplane noises," he warned the child.

"He's a big softie, Frankie. Give him a sad face, and he'll cave." Evelyn couldn't quite manage to hide her wide grin behind her coffee mug after that comment.

"I'll deal with you later," He gave her a mock scowl.

Frankie seemed to think his reaction was hilarious and kicked her feet, screaming "oftie" at the top of her lungs, giggling hysterically with every repeat of the word.

"Francesca."

Little Frankie had a stare-off with her mother, only conceding when Quentin intervened with a butterfly-soft tap to her tiny nose. "Listen to your mother, you little monster. The sooner you eat, the sooner we can play in Grandpa's toy room."

That did the trick, and Frankie gobbled down every spoonful presented to her.

"Parenting trick 101," Quentin said in an aside to Simon. "You'll need to remember that when you and Evelyn create little rug rats of your own."

Simon sought out Evelyn, but she was already engrossed in conversation with a stunning chocolate-haired woman on her right.

"That's Spring," Quentin volunteered. "And the male model next to her is Knox."

"Is he really a model?" Simon couldn't remember talk of anyone but Evelyn's cousin, Mackenzie, modeling as a profession.

"No," Holly said as she delivered a soft elbow to her husband's ribs. "This big lummox is jealous because Knox is prettier than he is."

"I'm getting a complex, my prickly pear. Keep it up." He popped another piece of croissant in her mouth to keep her from responding. "On a serious note, Knox has an off-the-charts IQ, rivaled only by Spring. The two of them are scary intelligent, and they seem to solve all the world's problems in half the time it takes the rest of us."

Simon had a clear understanding of why the couple had joined them for breakfast. An educated guess said they'd already been alerted to the soul-joining sexcapades he and Evelyn got up to last night. "Have they come up with a solution to our problem?"

"Yes and no," Holly replied for her husband.

"Yes, Spring knows what to do," Quentin said and paused for his wife to answer the next part.

"And, no, it isn't a simple fix," she dutifully inserted. "Isis will need to be summoned, and it's anyone's guess if she'll reverse what's been done."

Other than the threat to Evelyn's health, Simon wasn't upset by the turn of events last night. After he located Pete and dug up the evidence he needed to put the man behind bars for life, he intended to seek the Aether's help.

CHAPTER 22

$\mathcal{E}$velyn surreptitiously watched Simon as he interacted with Frankie. There was a softness in his face she'd never seen before, and the child's face sparkled as she babbled nonsense to the one adult who gave her his full attention. The sweet scene created an ache in Evelyn's heart. How long had he shut himself away from the world due to his curse and the requirements of his job? Since Tiffany's passing, or had it been before that?

"Do you want one of your own?" Spring asked her in a quiet voice, for Evelyn's ears alone.

Although in her forties, Evelyn's body was that of a much younger woman, thanks to magic and genetics. Forty-four was still within the child-bearing years for witches.

"I honestly don't know," she said. "Some days, I think it might be nice to have a few kids running underfoot. But I also enjoy my freedom and solitude. I have the sneaking suspicion I'd not have much quiet time after kids came along."

"Knox and I want to wait as long as possible, for those same reasons. It isn't a sin not to want children, you know."

Evelyn smiled and nodded, understanding the point her cousin was trying to make. "If we don't cure my faux pas from the stone circle, it will be a moot point. Also, Pete Wilson has become as slippery as an eel and dropped off our radar. I can't believe anyone not possessing magic has that capability."

"What has Martin come up with?"

"Not a damned thing. It's weird, don't you think? We have scrying, the WC, and every spell known to man at our disposal. I don't get it." Frustrated with their fruitless search, Evelyn shoved aside her plate and sat back in her seat with a huff. "I thought the Thorne way would be easier than the FBI's playbook."

"Is it possible he's dead?"

The thought never occurred to her. Disconcerted, she stared at Spring. "Holy crap! That has to be it. You're a gen—"

"Genius, yeah, I know." Spring said it like she was tired of hearing people sing her praises, and Evelyn laughed at her put-out tone.

"Girlfriend, if I looked like you, had half your magical talent, and a quarter of your smarts, I'd rule the world," she told her.

Spring rolled her eyes and reached for her fork. "You *do*. But like our dear cousin Piper, you prefer to do things the hard way."

With no real argument to the contrary, Evelyn shrugged. "Maybe you and I can spend more time together, and you can teach me what I'm missing."

"I'd love that. Also, I'll teach you how to blackmail Uncle Alastair into shopping trips in Paris." She raised her sweet voice for the last comment and sent a mischievous look in Alastair's direction. He responded with a wave of his hand, and a credit card appeared next to her plate. Laughing, Spring tucked it into her bra. "See? It works every time."

"Okay, hooker, let's go summon Isis and figure out what we have to do to break a soul-bond."

Simon looked up as Evelyn stood. "Should I take part?"

"It wouldn't be a bad idea if you were there," she replied. "Trevor and Alastair might want to take part as well. It's well-known Isis has a soft spot for our fearless family leader."

With a tender kiss to Frankie's temple, Simon gave her back to her father. "Thanks for sharing breakfast with me, Miss Frankie."

The toddler beamed her joy.

"You look jealous of a kid," Simon said after Evelyn joined him.

"I am." With a side-look and a half-smile, she said, "She's had all your attention this morning."

"Who knew you were so needy?" he teased.

"Apparently not me," she retorted as she laced her arm through his. "But you bring out the worst in me. On another note, is it possible Pete is dead, and whoever framed you is leading us on a wild-goose chase?"

He pulled her to the side of the dining-room door, out of the path of the others. "Explain."

"No amount of searching, scrying, or spells have turned up anything on him. If he were alive and kicking, Martin or Ryker should've found him by now."

"I don't know who would do that or what they'd have to gain from it." Simon ran a hand through his hair and sighed. "It never occurred to me that Pete isn't behind this."

"It makes more sense than him setting you up to take a fall. He was your mentor for years, Simon. Looking back, the affection he had for you didn't seem feigned."

"On another note, I talked to Trevor last night. We want to see the Aether at some point and have him remove what remains of my power. Eliminating the threat of death to others is high on my priority list."

Evelyn watched him for a reaction as she said, "Especially if Isis rejects our request to remove the bond, right?"

Their gazes connected, and in his eyes, she saw caring and concern. She also saw grim determination.

"If my Death Dealer toxicity can be neutralized, I'd like to consider keeping our bond in place," he said.

Her breath locked in her lungs. She hadn't expected him to reveal the truth this early, knowing how he felt about what he may have done to his wife and how reluctant he was to put Evelyn in jeopardy. All she could do was nod her agreement since the overabundance of love she was feeling had seized her throat. Her tears blurred his beloved face, and she blinked furiously, ducking her head to hide her reaction.

Simon tilted her chin up and kissed her with achingly sweet tenderness. "I said it, and I meant it, Evelyn. I love you."

"This is an about-face from yesterday," she managed in a relatively neutral voice.

"I've had all night to think about it, and I want you in my life if it's safe for you."

"I don't care if it is or isn't, Simon Says. Life is short and extremely unpredictable." She caressed his cheek. "If yesterday's bullet was a foot to the left, I wouldn't be here having this conversation with you."

He rested his forehead against hers. "Don't remind me."

"Come on. Let's see what Isis has to say."

CHAPTER 23

Simon walked with Evelyn to the clearing. It looked beautiful in the mid-morning light, and the serene sight gave him a sense of peace. The singing birds added a special ambience and lent to the wonder.

"It's easy to view this as the sacred place it is," she said, echoing Simon's thoughts.

He squeezed her hand in agreement.

They paused a few feet from the altar, and from the corner of his eye, he saw Evelyn grin.

"Stop, you troublemaker. I don't need everyone seeing my reaction to last night's memory," he scolded, trying his damnedest not to laugh.

"How did you know what I was thinking?"

"Deviltry is written all over your face. Prior to today, I wouldn't have said yours was expressive. You have hidden depths, Evelyn Thorne."

"I think you're simply more observant since you realized you love me."

He almost slipped and said he'd known he loved her for close to a year, but he caught himself in time. "Maybe," he murmured instead.

The rest of their group conversed a few feet away, and there were nods of agreement all around.

"I've never summoned a goddess. What do we need to do?" he asked Evelyn.

"I'm in the same boat, Simon Says. There's never been a need for me to talk to one."

In the end, the only person it required was Alastair Thorne. Being a descendent of Isis had its privileges, Simon supposed.

Other than a blinding white-gold light that seemed to vertically split the space in front of them, she showed up with little fanfare. To put it mildly, she was simply stunning. With hair a shimmering blue-black and kohl-lined tiger-like eyes, there was no mistaking her heritage as an Egyptian goddess. Her dress was a soft buttercream yellow and gave the illusion of being see-through, but in reality, it reflected the perfect amount of shimmer to provide modest coverage for her world-class curves. The dress draped over her left shoulder, held together with a jeweled clasp, and a gold serpent bangle balanced the look and graced her upper right arm. She looked exactly like the goddess she was.

Simon didn't realize his jaw was sagging until Evelyn tapped his chin with her index finger.

"You're catching flies," she whispered with a breathy chuckle.

"Sorry. I've never been this close to a deity, and now I know why temples were made in her honor."

"And you were worried about your reaction to last night's memory," she said dryly. "It's your reaction to a sexy goddess you have to be concerned with."

He hurriedly glanced down, horrified she might be serious. Once he took stock of his person, he gave her a glare. "Not cool."

"But funny, nonetheless." She released his hand and strode to where Spring and Knox had knelt to honor Isis. Falling to her knees, Evelyn bowed her head, gesturing wildly with her left arm for Simon to join her.

He didn't know what formalities were required, but he immediately dropped down beside her and copied her pose.

"You may all rise," Isis announced. "Death Dealer, please step forward."

Simon looked at Trevor but quickly realized all eyes were on *him*, including his brother's and Isis's. Inhaling a lungful of air, he complied and stopped a foot from her.

"You have a request of me, I understand," she said. Her smile was kind and her exotic eyes all-knowing.

Because Isis's ultimate decision affected Evelyn, too, he felt she should participate in their conversation. He half-turned, holding a hand out to her. Once she joined them, he faced Isis again. Her smile had widened, and the calculating look in her eye made him nervous as fuck.

"Evelyn and I unknowingly joined our souls last night on sacred land. We would like for you to remove the bond, Exalted One." He'd added the title because he'd heard Alastair say it a moment before when he'd summoned her.

Her gaze dropped to their joined hands and stayed focused there for a long, agonizing minute. When Simon thought he'd go mental with the wait, she met his gaze.

"No."

The breath Simon didn't know he was holding whooshed out, and a wave of dizziness assailed him.

Shit!

Panic for the future and all the possible outcomes played on repeat in his mind, and his hands grew clammy. He wanted to protest, but how did one argue with a goddess? How did he appeal to her softer side?

Turning her back, Isis strolled to the altar. "What you did together was an act of love," she said, her clear, accented voice ringing out around them. "The bond holds."

Dropping Evelyn's hand, Simon approached the altar. "My magic wasn't bound completely as a child, Exalted One. It has the potential to contaminate and kill those close to me. I can't have it happen to Evelyn like it did to my last wife." He didn't care that his voice sounded pleading. He'd beg if he had to. *"Please."*

"I'm not uncaring or unaware of the circumstances, Beloved." She touched his cheek. "However, I won't alter the Fates' plan for you. Balance must be kept in all things."

"What does that mean? Why can't you? Should Evelyn die for my ignorance and error in judgment?" His throat felt raw and scratchy, and his eyes stung. "I love her," he said raggedly. "Please don't do this to her. If someone has to pay for this, let it be me."

"You mistake me, Simon Blane. I didn't say I *cannot*, I said I *won't*. Should you solve the riddle of your current predicament, you and Evelyn will have a long and lovely life together. No illness will infect her."

It took a few precious seconds for the words to sink in, but he'd never experienced such a profound relief when they did. "To be clear, the 'current predicament' you refer to doesn't mean my Death Dealer abilities or lack thereof, but my mortal problem?"

Her beatific smile widened into a pleased grin as if he were the most brilliant of pupils. "Precisely. Well done, child." Leaning in, she imparted one last nugget of information. "The problem doesn't lie with you but with Benjamin Blane. His past deeds are circling back around."

Simon's stomach flipped. "I don't even know where to find him."

"The Aether does. And when you speak to him, you may tell him your full powers are to be restored to you. He need not ask the Authority. This comes down from higher up." She strode toward the golden rift, stopping a few feet from her destination. "Be well, my children. Blessed be."

As she crossed the plane from earth to the Otherworld, the light folded in on itself and sealed the gap.

Simon stared at the place she'd been standing as he tried to wade through what he'd learned and what it could possibly mean for his future. Gladness and gratitude filled his heart, and he spun around in time to catch Evelyn as she rushed toward him. He hugged her so tightly, he feared he'd snap her spine, but she didn't protest. She held on to him just as hard.

CHAPTER 24

The Dethridge estate was more impressive than Alastair Thorne's, but also a lot more gothic in appearance. Where Alastair's place was the picture of modern architecture, the Aether's grand home was centuries old, dating back to who knew when. To Simon's untrained American eye, it resembled a castle. All stone and floor-to-ceiling windows. Turrets and carefully crafted arches. Sprawling steps led up to a set of massive double doors. The grounds were all well-manicured, and mighty English oak trees dotted the landscape as far as the eye could see.

"It's a helluva lot more majestic than Downton Abbey," he muttered.

Next to him, Evelyn snorted. But a quick glance showed Trevor was equally impressed by the grandeur of the old place.

"Who knew you watched Downton Abbey?" Evelyn said with a light laugh.

"Tiff's favorite show." Simon was beginning to feel weird bringing up his ex-wife at every turn. It felt like a betrayal of both women. Like he was measuring them, when in fact, he wasn't. He simply had no other frame of reference. Tiffany had been with him since he was a kid.

As if sensing his turmoil, Evelyn clasped his hand in her light, comforting way. "I know. She made me watch it often enough when you were working late." With a nod toward the imposing entrance of the house, she asked, "Think they have a Mr. Carson?"

Her teasing broke through Simon's tension, and he grinned. "I'd be disappointed if they didn't."

Before they reached the steps, the doors opened, and a black-haired child skipped out. Her dress was stained with what looked to be chocolate, and her hair was tied up in mismatched ponytails. The same food circled her smiling mouth.

"Hello," she said. "Papa will be here soon, and he gets cross with me if I tell what I know, so I have to be quick." Although she couldn't have been more than seven or eight, her tone was eerily adult-like. "I'm only telling you this because you're Mack's family, and I love Mack."

Simon turned his head to look at Evelyn, and her stupefied expression said it all.

"Who are you?" he asked the child.

"I'm Sabrina. Mack likes to call me the Baby Aether." A grin lit up her adorable elfin-like features. "I'm an Oracle."

Having no idea what the hell that was, Simon half-turned to his brother for answers.

Trevor's expression was also mystified, so there was no answer there.

"I don't know what that is," Simon admitted to the girl.

She shrugged. "I see things."

"What do we need to know before your dad comes?"

"The man who wants to hurt you blames your dad for his family —"

"Beastie!"

A momentary chagrin turned her grin into a grimace, but the little girl rallied and pasted on a wide, welcoming smile for the man approaching from behind her. She spun around and held up her arms.

He complied and picked her up, unmindful of her ruined clothing.

"I was greeting our guests, Papa," she told him pertly. "They're here to find answers, so I—"

"Disobeyed the no-revealing-the-future rule?" Damian Dethridge said dryly.

His affection for his lively daughter wasn't in question. One had only to watch them together for an instant to see their deep, abiding love for each other. They had an unbreakable father-daughter bond, and the sight caused a yearning in Simon's chest. Before that moment, he'd never much thought of children, but some basic, paternal need kicked in as he witnessed their hug.

"It's the energy they put off," Evelyn explained quietly. "You can't help but be caught up in the feeling."

"Well, that explains it," he muttered.

Damian summed them up with one look, gave his precocious daughter a kiss on the cheek, and placed her back on solid ground. "Go find your mother and leave our guests to me, Beastie. And no more gelato until after dinner."

"Will you tell them, Papa? Evelyn is Mack's cousin, and Mack is our family now." Sabrina seemed worried they should know whatever news she intended to impart.

What amazed Simon was that the Aether understood precisely what she meant, and the man nodded.

"I promise to help them in any way I can, my love. Run along."

"Thank you, Papa!"

Sabrina's happy smile caused a tightness in Simon's chest, and he wanted to promise the child the moon and stars. "Christ, she packs a punch."

His low-voiced comment shouldn't have traveled to Damian's ears, but the man faced him all the same. "That she does, Mr. Blane. That she does."

"How did you… uh… how… you *heard* me?"

The Aether smiled, and his grin was as impactful as his kid's. "Not with my ears, Simon Blane." He tapped his temple. "In here. Your thoughts were loud enough for me to hear."

Simon froze. *Was the man saying he was a mind reader, for fuck's sake?*

"Only when it pertains to my daughter."

The words never left Damian's mouth, but Simon heard them in his head all the same.

"You're telepathic?"

"To a large degree," the Aether acknowledged aloud.

"Alastair sends his regards," Evelyn finally said when she reached the top of the exterior stairs. Her voice was breathy, and her eyes had a star-struck quality to them.

Damian's warm smile flashed, and he clasped her hands in his. "When you see him again, please tell him I'm sorry he couldn't join us. But it's a pleasure to finally meet you, Evelyn Thorne. Mack has told us many wonderful stories about you."

The man oozed charm.

Simon's new dilemma was whether to hate the guy for his sheer perfection or whether to admire the hell out of him.

The Aether's shrewd obsidian eyes shifted to him. "Admiration is always better than hate, Mr. Blane."

"Admiration it is, but can you give Evelyn her hands back now?" he returned, careful to bank his jealous thoughts so he didn't spoil their entire fact-finding mission.

Damian grinned and held out his hand for Simon to shake. *"When you meet my wife, it will put you at ease."*

"Stay out of my head, please."

"Habit."

"What did I miss?" Evelyn asked as her worried gaze darted between the two of them.

Trevor finally broke his silence. "They are holding a telepathic conversation, unless I miss my guess."

All friendliness left Damian as he turned his attention to Trevor. "Death Dealer."

"Aether."

"I know why your brother and Ms. Thorne are here, but what brings you to my door?"

"I'm here to ensure my brother stays alive long enough to clear his name." Trevor's tone was cold and no-nonsense, and rarely had Simon ever heard him speak in that manner.

"Trev," he said warningly. "We're just here for answers."

"And to get your power restored," his brother reminded him. "What Isis so handily failed to mention was the restoration process isn't always cut and dried."

Damian watched Simon carefully when he said, "Your brother is correct, Mr. Blane. Infusing your body with the power of a Death Dealer might very well end your life. Likely it won't, but it could."

CHAPTER 25

*E*velyn thought she might pass out when the Aether dropped his little bombshell. She gripped Simon's forearm to steady her weak legs.

"Why?" she demanded. "He's a natural-born Death Dealer. Why would it kill him to have his power returned?"

Simon's tension could be felt in the clenched muscle under her hand. He looked calm as fuck, and the only way she'd have guessed his inner turmoil was because of her touch.

"We'll discuss all of it in due time," Damian assured her. "First, let me welcome you all to my home. Come, I'm sure Vivian will have put the kettle on and conjured refreshments."

Sure enough, as they entered a parlor off the main hall, a willowy woman with upswept, icy-white hair was setting out a tea set and a plate of cookies. When she straightened from her chore, she placed a hand on her protruding belly and offered a polite smile.

"Sabrina told me we had company," she said. Her gaze didn't warm as it settled on her husband, but she couldn't quite hide her caring. Perhaps it was the hint of sadness in her eyes when Vivian looked at the Aether, or maybe Evelyn was mistaking sadness for longing, but a more profound and harder to define emotion lurked in his wife's guarded gaze.

Evelyn knew all too well the need to keep her feelings in check, so she crossed the room in her brisk, FBI manner and held out a hand in greeting. "I'm Evelyn Thorne."

"Vivian Stephens… or uh, Dethridge."

"We've been married for over a decade, Viv. I'd have thought you'd have remembered your last name by now." His tone had a hard edge but also a tinge of hurt.

Up close, Evelyn saw firsthand the color sweep into Vivian's cheeks and the compression of her lips.

"Don't be an ass, sweetheart," the woman said coolly. "It was a slip of the tongue. These things happen. We've only been reunited a short while."

Their gazes locked. Obsidian and ice blue. Challenge crackled in the air between them. Surprisingly, Damian was the first to look away.

"I apologize."

Evelyn wasn't sure to whom he was apologizing, but Vivian sighed. To Evelyn's mind, the sound was frustrated and bordered sad.

"I'll leave you to it."

"You're American," she blurted when it sunk in the other woman didn't have an accent.

The first genuine warmth filled Vivian's eyes as she released a light laugh. "Yes. Born and bred on a private, uncharted island off the coast of Cape Cod, Massachusetts."

"How is it possible there are any private, uncharted islands off the coast of—" Simon abruptly ended his question as the rest of them turned to stare at him, not bothering to hide their amusement. He held up a hand and gave Evelyn a rueful grin. "Sorry. Forgot I was dealing with a bunch of witches. Cloaking. I get it."

"It's named Serafina Island after my three-times great-grandmother, Serafina Stephens," Vivian told them. "My sisters still live in our family home on the island."

Evelyn's curiosity spiked, and she was compelled to ask, "How in the world did you two meet if you're American and your husband is English?"

"Actually, I grew up in America," Damian said. "Nathanial Thorne and his wife—your namesake Evelyn—took me in when I was a boy." His face softened when he looked at his wife. "I saw Vivian at some mandatory Council meeting or other and never looked at anyone else." He quickly shuttered the insight to his deeper feelings with a half-smile and a shrug. "I'm afraid I didn't give her much of a choice. I set out to seduce her into marriage from the moment we met."

He picked up a cookie, inspected it, and took a bite. It was difficult not to notice that he avoided meeting his wife's eyes after he'd imparted the information. Almost as if he feared seeing rejection.

"Well, that's a truly romantic story," Evelyn said brightly, then winced at her stupid-ass comment. These two were obviously at a rough patch in their marriage, and here she was babbling about romance and love. She had both on the brain lately.

Vivian surprised her with a quick hug. "You're as lovely as your cousin Mackenzie, Ms. Thorne. I hope you'll come back for a visit when you have more time."

"I'd like that," Evelyn agreed. "Shall I pour so we can get down to business?"

"I'll leave you to it," Vivian said. She paused in passing her husband but didn't reach for him in any way. "I'll try to keep Sabrina occupied and out of your business matters for a bit."

"Thank you." Damian's voice had deepened, and once again, his expression softened as he looked down at his wife. "I shan't be long."

"Take your time. There's more gelato to make for tonight's dessert. We have to replace what she's already eaten."

He grinned and watched her until she left the room.

"Your wife is incredibly sweet," Evelyn said as she bent over the tea set and began to pour. "I like her."

"She likes you, too. But don't be fooled by her angelic looks. Sabrina got her devilish nature from her mother." He declined tea and gestured for Simon and Trevor to sit.

"I'll get right to the point of Sabrina's aborted revelation.

Benjamin Blane made a vicious enemy roughly three decades ago, and now the man has discovered your father had children. His goal is to destroy everything Ben cares about. The three of you included."

The Blane brothers sat in shocked silence. Evelyn couldn't blame them. That was a lot for Damian to unpack in three sentences.

"But I've never met Simon's father," she protested. "Why target me?"

Damian crossed to the far side of the room to a sideboard with crystal bottles and glass tumblers. He poured three drinks and carried them back, handing off one to each of them. "Brandy. Top shelf. You may need the fortification."

Because she wanted a clear head, Evelyn only put a dash into her existing cup of tea. As she lifted it to sip, she caught Damian watching her. The light of appreciation was in his dark eyes. It didn't seem sexual but more affectionate in nature.

"What?"

"You remind me of Evie. She was strong and brave—like you."

"But you don't know me."

His smile widened, and this time his amusement caused the fine lines on either side of his eyes to crinkle.

She caught her breath. Never had she seen so gorgeous a creature in all her life. Yes, she loved Simon, but *damn*. She was certainly a female first.

Abruptly he grew serious as if he sensed the effect he had and felt the need to cut it off at the knees. Somewhere along the way, she'd heard his mother was an Enchantress, and Evelyn could easily see the mother's seductive powers had been passed to the son.

"Okay, back to the Blanes," she said. "Our goals are to restore Simon's power and find his father to eliminate the big baddie. What do we need to do to get this show on the road?"

The men laughed.

Simon placed a hand on her knee and squeezed. "My practical Evelyn," he said softly.

"Always."

CHAPTER 26

Simon hadn't missed Evelyn's reaction to the Aether, and he also hadn't missed Damian shut that shit right down. The guy wasn't out to charm women despite his natural magnetism.

Simon finally understood their telepathic conversation on the stairs.

"Do you know where my father is, Mr. Dethridge?" he asked.

"I generally stay out of matters not concerning my family directly unless I'm called on by the Authority or the Witches' Council. However, if anyone possesses powers like your family's, Mr. Blane, I make it a point to keep track of them."

"Where is he?"

"He went into seclusion in Ireland."

"Seclusion?" Trevor's tone was sharp, and Simon sat straighter.

He had no idea why his brother would take exception to the word, but he obviously did. Damian's expression didn't alter, yet somehow, he conveyed grimness. Whatever "seclusion" was, it wasn't good.

Evelyn put down her teacup and linked her hand with Simon's. "Okay, I'll bite. What does it mean for a Death Dealer to go into seclusion?"

"It means Dad is being held against his will in a remote Authority stronghold," Trevor explained. Outrage radiated off him, and he glared at Damian as if it were all his fault. For all Simon knew, it could be, but he decided to withhold his judgment until it was confirmed.

"My understanding is he volunteered to go. He was in a bad state after your mother died and needed to regroup before he hurt someone."

Surging to his feet, fists balled, Trevor turned all his fury on Damian. "It's little more than a prison camp," he shouted.

"Calm down, Blane. Ben came to me, seeking help. The Irish stronghold was his idea."

"You're a liar! He wouldn't leave his family without a word all these years."

Simon rose and placed firm pressure on his brother's chest to prevent him from doing anything foolish. The Aether could wipe the floor with both of them by simply waving a hand. "Trev…"

A memory he wasn't aware he possessed floated to the surface of his mind. He dropped his arm and turned around to face Damian. "*You!* I remember you! Earlier in the night, right before my dad supposedly died, you were at our house. I don't know why I didn't recall before."

It seemed like something he'd remember, considering how trau-matized he was by the loss of his father.

"Yes. Ben requested I wipe your memory of the visit. He didn't want you to figure out his demise was all a ruse." The Aether left them to pour himself a drink, and he downed it in one gulp. Taking time to refill his glass, he allowed them to process what they'd learned.

Question after question flooded Simon's mind, and he tried to wade through to get to the most relevant to their situation. All the others could wait until he saw his father again. "Who is the enemy, and how do we stop him?"

"I'll let Ben explain when you see him." With a challenging brow in Trevor's direction, Damian said, "About twenty-five years ago, he left the bonds of seclusion. But he fell in love with Ireland and built a home just outside of Roscommon. I believe he thought it would be a good place to hide from the outside world."

Simon could hardly believe he would see his father again. If the situation weren't dire, he might've waited until his emotions were in check. What he would say to his dad after three and a half decades was anyone's guess.

"We can go when you're ready, Simon," Damian said, not unkindly. "You're all safe here until you decide your next move."

"Do you mind if I step out for some air?"

"Not at all." He placed his tumbler on the sideboard. "I have a few things to see to. Not the least of which is to make sure the Beastie hasn't convinced her mother she needs another vat of chocolate gelato to eat."

Simon appreciated the attempt at levity, and he smiled his thanks.

He waited until the Aether cleared the entrance before turning on his heel and heading for the French doors. Right before he reached them, they swung open. It gave him pause.

Was this house haunted, or were there cloaked servants roaming the place?

"Simon!"

He waited, not turning until Evelyn reached his side. "I need a few minutes to clear my head. I won't be long." He toyed with a wavy lock of her hair, mainly to avoid her too-observant gaze. "You'll be all right with Trev for a bit?"

"Of course. But I'm here if you need to talk." She rose on her toes and pressed her lips to his in a light, affectionate manner. "I'll be here," she reiterated.

There was a deeper meaning, and it harkened back to the dark days after Tiffany's passing. Minus the kiss, this scene was reminiscent of when he was at his lowest point.

Simon lowered his forehead to hers and touched noses with her. "I don't deserve you," he whispered.

"Sure you do. You're awesome," she said with a tender smile.

Because he wanted to crush her in an embrace and never let her go, he shifted back. "See you in ten."

CHAPTER 27

As Trevor watched the interplay between Simon and Evelyn, his heart contracted painfully in his chest. He hated to see his little brother hurting. Hated. It! But that's what their selfish prick of a father had done by leaving a small child to fend for himself after enrolling his elder son into the Authority's brutal boot camp.

Now, Simon was the target of a Machiavellian plot against Benjamin Blane from some past deed of their father's. Trevor wanted to spit nails and wipe out all those involved.

He joined Evelyn by the doors, and together they watched Simon jog across the terrace and down the stone steps. Her worried expression mirrored Trevor's internal feelings.

"You told me he's strong enough to handle all of this," Trev reminded her.

"He is." She abruptly faced him. "It's not your brother I'm truly concerned about. It's how this is all going to play out. What is the endgame here? What could your father have possibly done to get on this man's shit list?"

"I don't know. I never recalled hearing a whisper of anything in the past." But the suspicion surrounding their aunt's shooting had never gone away. Trevor was left to wonder if she'd been a victim of more than circumstances.

"You've thought of something."

"Yes. But I'll confirm it with our father before I spout off at the mouth about things I don't know for sure."

"Always a good plan to hold your cards close to your chest. But make sure you give me a heads-up if you're holding all the aces, okay?"

She surprised a laugh out of him. "I like you, Evelyn Thorne."

"I like you, too, Trevor Blane." She steered him back toward the sitting area. "Help me eat all these cookies. I suspect food is going to be the last thing on anyone's mind later."

"Don't I know it."

Damian Dethridge watched Simon Blane meander through the garden two stories below. The man's conflict wasn't small by any means. Hope, love, fear, anger, frustration—it had all been there when they'd discussed Ben.

Damian had remembered Simon from the beginning. He'd been a bright, happy child. And, not too dissimilar from Sabrina earlier, young Simon had been wearing his ice cream over half his face. His enthusiasm for his treat had taken over the basic manners he'd been taught, and he downed the ice cream with an enthusiasm only a child could express.

Later that same night, his large blue eyes had lost their happiness, and he'd become frightened by what he'd accidentally overheard in the study of the Blane house.

"*Dutch won't stop until you're all dead, Blane,*" Damian said. "*You should've told the Authority to go fuck themselves when they assigned you to the case.*"

"*I didn't know how lethal he was until I was neck-deep in it.*" Ben stared at the window and scrubbed the heel of his hand over his heart. "*How was I to know he'd figure it out?*"

Two-and-a-half years was a long time to remain undercover as someone's bodyguard, and they all knew he'd been playing a game of chance.

Joining Ben on the far side of the room, Damian clapped a hand on his shoulder. "You know, the easiest solution is to remove Dutch from the playing field. It won't bring back Gloria, but your boys will be safe, as will your sister."

"I've taken too much from him, Dethridge. Too damned much."

The raw agony in Ben's voice gave him pause.

"And he didn't retaliate with Gloria's death?"

The wave of guilt from Ben hit Damian like a tsunami.

"What am I missing?" he demanded with a hard edge to his voice.

A shrug and a sip of his cocktail was all the answer Ben would give.

"Blane, I'm not fucking around here. You can tell me, or I can do a mind dive, but I need to know to protect you."

"I was involved with Dutch's wife before I followed the orders to take her life and that of his daughter."

After all the years Damian had spent in this world, there was little left to shock him. But Benjamin Blane had managed it.

"But you loved Gloria..." Words wouldn't come, but the anger and disappointment did. Some spouses cheated. The fact couldn't be denied, but Damian had expected better from his friend. "What the hell, Blane?" he growled.

Ben winced and hissed in a breath from the magical smack of the Aether power.

"You knew Dutch was mafia and a kingpin in the mortal world. You must bloody well know they don't forget a slight against them. But you still shoved aside your common sense, fucked his wife, then killed her anyway? To add insult to injury, you added his daughter to your hit list." Damian stalked away to pace, so he didn't give in to the overwhelming temptation to strangle the living shit out of Ben. He'd made a half trip around the study's interior when the truth hit him. "He's discovered what you are, hasn't he?"

"Yes. I believe so."

With a suddenness that gave him a blinding headache, Damian received image after image of Gloria's tortured-filled day. It played out like a movie in his mind, and it took a concerted effort not to lose the contents of his stomach as he experienced a small fraction of her pain and bore witness to the grizzly details.

"He did," Damian confirmed flatly. "He extracted the truth from her in ways you don't want to learn about."

"I have to protect my boys from him. Please help me."

And that was the crux of the matter; no matter how much Ben might deserve whatever Dutch doled out, the Blane boys didn't.

"Benjamin Blane will die tonight," Damian stated.

The third presence in the room made itself known. "Nooooo!"

Damian wasn't certain how he'd missed the boy's sugared-up energy, but little Simon's traumatized face said he'd heard everything. Tears streamed down his pale cheeks, and he stared in horror at Ben and Damian.

A single nod from Ben granted Damian permission to remove the child's memory of their conversation. He withdrew to allow Ben his final goodbyes with the boy. Through the opening of the room across the hall, he could see the two hug and Simon smile up at his father as if the sun rose and set with him. The love of a child for a parent was unbreakable in most cases. Only a dastardly deed or purposefully inflicted pain could diminish it.

And as Damian observed adult Simon now, he understood the small boy was still inside, struggling to understand the forgotten moments the Aether unlocked during their conversation.

Damian didn't feel bad for restoring Simon's memories. The truth would help him in the coming days.

CHAPTER 28

"Ireland is colder than a witch's tit!" Trevor grumbled as he rubbed his hands together.

Evelyn gasped, then laughed. "I take exception to that, Trevor Blane."

"Yeah, quit being a little bitch, Trev. At least you have the magic to warm your cells. Some of us don't have that much." Simon wrapped an arm around Evelyn's waist and leaned in to whisper, "Personally, I don't think your tits are cold."

His comment brought her back to the other night in the clearing, and warmth rushed through her entire body. "They aren't when you hug me and whisper things of that nature," she replied.

From behind, Trevor nudged Simon. "Okay, lovebirds, can we get in out of the wind, please?"

They entered a pub called Lucky O'Malley's and found a table close to the back. On stage, a man strummed and sang a naughty little tune with his gaze locked on someone behind Evelyn. Curiosity got the better of her, and she turned to see what had caught his attention.

She gasped her joy. "I'll be damned."

"What?" Simon paused in the act of hanging his jacket over the back of the chair. "Everything okay?"

"Yep." She jumped up and kissed his cheek. "I suspect I know why Damian suggested we meet here, though. Be right back."

Evelyn stopped a few feet from the bar top and waited for the dark-haired woman to quit making eyes at the singer long enough to notice her. A squeal rang out the second she did. Stopping only long enough to slap a mug of beer in front of a customer, her cousin Piper closed the distance at a run. The two women hugged, pulled away to laugh, and embraced a second time.

"What are you doing here, cuz?" Piper sandwiched Evelyn's face between her palms and shook her head. "Gah, gorgeous as ever, without trying. And here I look like a swamp rat."

"Oh, shut up. You know you could never look bad. The proof is in that hot Irish dude's eyes."

Piper turned and smiled at the man in question. "Yep. He's my fiancé, Cian." Leaning into Evelyn, she flashed an emerald and diamond ring, but her eyes were still locked on the singer. "Isn't he dreamy?"

"Definite fantasy-inducing material," Evelyn agreed. "I'm here on a fact-finding mission, but when I'm done, will you have time to catch up? I feel like we haven't talked in an age."

"Absolutely. Cian's family owns O'Malley's Black Cat Inn, right next door. It's the slow season, and we have plenty of room if you want to stay over."

"I'd like that. I haven't been to Ireland in years."

"Good. You can tell me all about the intense man who can't stop staring at your ass."

Sparing a glance over her shoulder, Evelyn met Simon's appreciative look. His exaggerated wink caused a bubble of laughter to burst from her.

"That's Simon."

"Your *boss*, Simon?"

"*Ex*-boss, and yes, he's part of my latest mission." She faced Piper and grinned.

"Mmm, nice. Is it *undercover*-work?"

The twinkle in Piper's honey eyes did Evelyn in, and she lost her fight with laughter. "Since when did you become the one throwing out innuendoes left and right? I thought that gig belonged to Liz and Mack."

"Since him."

The music stopped, and after a quick quip for the crowd, Cian jumped down from the stage and headed straight for them.

"Crikey, Pip, he's even better up close."

"Right?"

When he reached them, he bent Piper back and kissed her with so much passion, Evelyn needed to fan her face. For sure, Piper's wits were scattered when he set her back on her feet because she couldn't seem to remember Evelyn's name when Cian asked.

"You'll have to forgive my darlin' Piper," he told her. "She's easily overcome."

Flushing a brilliant scarlet, an indication Cian wasn't far off the mark, Piper elbowed him in the ribs. "Shut it and go serve up these louts in your pub."

"You become more like Bridget every day, Piper me love. I'll be limiting the time you spend with her, to be sure."

"Go!"

With a chuckle and a hearty smack on her ass, he sauntered behind the bar. Once there, he threw a towel over his shoulder and placed his hands on his lean hips. "Who'll be wanting a pint of plain?" he called out.

Four hands shot up.

"This place is awesome, Pip. *Cian* is awesome," Evelyn said to her.

"I love it, and him." Her eyes glowed with adoration as she watched the object of her affection joke and laugh with his patrons. "He's perfect for me."

"I can see that."

The air shifted, became denser and packed with energy. All eyes turned toward the entrance.

"Wow," Piper whispered. "Don't look now, but the Aether just walked through the door."

"He's here for us." As Evelyn watched him survey his surroundings, she realized they were likely to receive unwanted attention. Damian had the draw of an Enchantress, and others desired to see and be seen by him. "Do you have a private room, by any chance?"

"Yes. Right through those double doors. It's closed off to our main customers unless there's a large party. You're welcome to use it." She patted Evelyn's shoulder. "I'll be in for your drink order after you all get settled. You might want to utilize Granny Thorne's cloaking spell. Hopefully, it will mitigate the interest in his presence."

"Thanks."

As Evelyn approached Damian, she studied the man next to him. He bore no resemblance to Simon or Trevor, and she was left to wonder if he'd adopted a disguise.

"Mr. Dethridge."

He smiled down at her. "Call me Damian, please. You've arranged a private room." It wasn't a question but a statement of fact. A shiver chased the length of her spine, and she realized she didn't care to have him pluck all her thoughts from her brain. "This way."

After they were secure from the prying eyes and ears of others, Damian shut the doors with a snap. The single word he spoke wasn't one Evelyn was familiar with. "What enchantment did you put in place?"

"Not only does it cloak us, but no one other than your cousin and her mate will remember we were here."

"Handy," she murmured her approval. "Remind me to get that spell from you later."

With a soul-warming chuckle and a light touch to her middle back, he guided her to a chair. "Please, allow me to introduce you to Benjamin Blane."

The glamour fell away to reveal an older version of Simon. The only difference being his cold, lifeless eyes. Where Simon's and his brother's were a lighter blue, Ben's were a flat gray, as if all color had been leeched out.

Here was a very miserable man. One with little hope for the future.

"Mr. Blane." She nodded politely but didn't offer her hand, fearing his touch would be as cool as a corpse.

A mere nod was his acknowledgment.

Cold bastard.

It might have been some inner instinct of hers, but she knew Benjamin Blane was dead inside. Whether from the Authority or from a lack of love and friendship, she didn't care to know.

Other than a simple, "It's good to see you, boys," he didn't bother to display any fatherly warmth.

Evelyn's heart ached for them. She didn't always see eye to eye with her parents, but she didn't doubt their love.

"Tell them about Dutch, Blane. They deserve to know," Damian instructed in a neutral tone.

There had been a flicker of something in Benjamin's eyes, and the air around them crackled with tension. It told Evelyn that Ben didn't want to be here, but the Aether wasn't giving him a choice in the matter.

As the story unfolded, she shot furtive glances in Simon's direction. His bland expression was reminiscent of times when he took statements from criminals, and he gave none of his thoughts away. Never once during Ben's monologue had Simon looked her way, and her worry began to build.

CHAPTER 29

Simon's thoughts were a jumbled mess. His father scarcely resembled the loving man he'd remembered from his childhood and looked like a shell of his former self. The distance in his eyes was frightening. He was a man ready to check out and who didn't give two fucks about the rest of the world. How the Aether managed to drag him here was a mystery.

Across from him, Evelyn's misery was building. Only someone familiar with her moods could tell, but her brain would be racing a mile a minute as she summed up the reactions of everyone present, himself included.

Benjamin Blane's tale was fantastical. Thrust into the dark world of a supernatural assassin by his own father, he'd done the same when the Authority demanded it of Trevor. Ben's undercover work had cost them both a mother and an aunt. By the gray hue of his brother's face, Simon had no doubt Trevor was seeing himself as Ben thirty years down the road. But Simon would be damned if he let that be Trev's fate. Somehow he'd find a way to intervene.

"Okay, let's take it down to basics," Evelyn said. "So we're all clear, this Dutch character is out for blood. Primarily Simon's and Trevor's, but he's willing to take out anyone in their general vicinity if it comes to that. All because you infiltrated his criminal ring, slept with his wife, and carried out an assassination for the Authority of said wife. You topped that shit sundae by killing his beloved daughter." She glared at Ben, and Simon was hard pressed not to smile at her fierceness. His Evelyn hated injustice. "I'm not missing anything, right? Like you didn't take out the family dog while you were at it, did you?"

A flicker of amusement lit Ben's eyes, giving momentary life to them before they dulled again. "No, Ms. Thorne. You haven't missed anything."

"Why were you in seclusion?" Trevor demanded. Torment was just below the surface of his anger, and Simon wondered if his brother was worried about going down the same path.

"A Death Dealer can't be left to wander aimlessly when he no longer has the desire to do their bidding. They are put in Authority rehab, and if they can't be made to see reason, their abilities are stripped away," Ben explained in a monotone voice.

"And you?" Simon asked, careful to keep it neutral. "Were yours stripped, or were you rehabbed?"

"Neither. They tasked me with cleaning up the mess I made. However, try as I might, I can't get close to Dutch. He's gone underground and surrounded himself with Blockers."

Simon addressed Damian, knowing the Aether would tell the truth. "What are Blockers?"

"They are sell-out witches and warlocks," Evelyn answered for him. "For a price, they will work together against their own kind. Usually to block powers in a perilous situation."

"You've had experience with them." Simon didn't need to ask. Her distaste with the subject said it all.

She answered anyway. "My family has. We almost lost a few of our number along the way because they couldn't use their magic or teleport."

"I find it hard to believe a Thorne was ever powerless," Ben said with a disbelieving snort.

"Believe it," she snapped. "But none of that matters now, Mr. Blane. You've put your sons in the crosshairs of a madman, a kingpin at that. And Simon doesn't have the magical means to protect himself."

Ben's head whipped in his direction. "Your power was to be restored. It was the one condition I demanded when I allowed those bastards to lock me up."

"Someone should've reminded them of that." Simon spread his hands wide. "I got nothing."

Rage made his father's eyes bluer, and purpose radiated from him when he stood abruptly. He addressed Damian. "We've got to get his abilities back, or he's a dead man walking, Dethridge. I have too many enemies."

"It will be done, Ben. But the most pressing matter is Dutch. I can neutralize Blockers, but I won't kill for you. You'll clean up your own mess."

"Of course. It was never in doubt."

Evelyn held up a hand as she rose to her feet. "Hold your roll, pops. This isn't a matter of going Dirty Harry on the mafia. This is a matter of clearing Simon's name. To do that, we need to find Pete Wilson. That's who we believe set him up."

Ben looked at Simon in confusion.

"Pete is my boss at the Bureau. Alastair Thorne has his crew digging, but there's no sign of him. We believe Pete set me up to look like the head of a criminal organization." He rubbed the back of his neck to ease the tight muscles. "Dutch's, if I'm not mistaken. I just don't know why."

Closing his eyes and dropping his chin to his chest, Ben released a weary sigh. "Pete Wilson is the nephew of Dutch's deceased wife. I had no idea he'd managed to secure a prime position with the FBI."

"He's the one who recruited me." Simon locked eyes with Evelyn across the distance of the table. "I find it hard to believe it was a twenty-plus-year setup, don't you?"

"I do. He seemed to genuinely like you, Simon."

"Perhaps he only found out who you were more recently," Damian suggested. "Other than to reveal what Ben was, Gloria never spoke the names of you or your brother. You were protected for the most part."

"Dutch never knew me as Benjamin Blane." His father crossed the room and placed his forearm on the mantle, staring down into the dancing flames of the hearth. "Gloria only became caught up in the mess when she came looking for me. Her timing was off, and she stumbled into Dutch's path instead."

Trevor jumped up and stalked to Ben's side. "Why did she not teleport the hell out of there?"

"I don't know, son. We'll never know."

"Only a threat to a loved one would make a woman sacrifice herself," Evelyn replied. Walking over to Simon, she ran a hand through his hair and smiled softly. "She would've done anything to protect her sons."

"You think they threatened us, and she gave herself willingly?"

"It's what I'd have done. But they had to know what her weakness was."

"I never mentioned my wife or children," Ben said with a shake of his head. "Ever."

"And yet they immediately knew who she was," she argued. "They had to surmise if you had a wife, it was possible you had kids. Perhaps Dutch bluffed."

The urge to hold someone, to stop being the island unto himself, hit Simon hard, and he drew Evelyn down into his lap for the much-needed human contact. Without question or comment, Evelyn leaned back against him and rested her hands atop his. Only she could chase away the chill permeating his soul.

"So the next step is to discover how Pete eventually discovered who I was and why he decided to use that knowledge against me," Simon stated.

"Your father essentially murdered his aunt. That's the why." Evelyn cast a sharp look in Ben's direction. "The how is what makes me curious. It wasn't as if witches have a witness protection agency that can be compromised."

The entire time they bounced around the conversation, the Aether had remained relatively quiet. When he rose to his feet, all the attention shifted to him. "There's a leak at the Authority. It's the only reasonable explanation."

Trevor turned positively white. "I think it's me."

CHAPTER 30

"**W**hat the fuck, Trev?"

"This past year, I met someone. A fellow witch." Trevor frowned as he thought about Deni and recalled their past. Not only had they been lovers, but they'd also been confidants. "For seven months, we were an item until she disappeared one day."

"When was that? And why didn't you look for her?" Evelyn asked.

"Three months ago. And I have. She simply disappeared, and the Trackers I employed haven't been able to find her." An ugly suspicion melded with unease in the pit of Trevor's stomach, and he fought his body's urge to lose the Guinness he consumed earlier. The similarity to Pete Wilson's disappearance was made more obvious.

"What did you tell her?" Simon's sickly expression matched what Trevor was feeling.

"Everything. Or as much as I knew." He scrubbed a hand over his face. "I thought at the time, she'd… we'd…" He trailed off and sighed. Who cared why he'd done it; the point was, he had. Knowing he was likely the one to put his brother in jeopardy didn't sit well.

Damian rubbed a spot between his perfect black brows. "And when you reencounter her, Mr. Blane—and trust me, it will happen—what is your intent?"

"What do you mean? Do you know something?" Hope mingled with fear. If the Aether was expecting Trevor to take Deni's life, a wrong for a wrong, the man was mistaken. He could no more hurt her than he could Simon.

Yes, Trevor had followed the Authority's dictates, but only to protect Simon from being drawn into the magical shitstorm the Fates liked to whip up every so often. He wouldn't kill for the sake of killing, and he didn't take a life without making sure it was for a damned good cause. Also, Deni had meant something to him. The first person in a long while.

"I know plenty. But rarely do I involve myself in matters of this nature. The only reason I'm doing so now is because Alastair Thorne would make my life miserable if anything happened to Evelyn, and by extension, her mate." His obsidian eyes touched on the couple in question. "For them, I will help you."

Trevor nodded his understanding. "We now know all the moving parts and the why of it. Next, we need a game plan to restore Simon's life back to normal. Mine and Benjamin's don't matter." And he meant it. He'd gladly forfeit his father's and/or his own to give his little brother back the one he deserved.

"Don't say that, Trev." Simon eased Evelyn from his lap and crossed to where he stood. The panic on his brother's handsome face tugged at Trevor's heart. He'd lost so much. Evelyn's was the only worthwhile relationship Simon possessed, and Trevor intended to make sure it lasted.

"It's true, Si. What is mine against all the good you and Evelyn do for others? I'm a mindless soldier for an archaic organization that removes free will. What's the point anymore?"

Simon had no answer, and his helplessness made Trevor sad.

As his older brother mentally firmed up whatever harebrained notion he had, a warning bell sounded in Simon's brain. Trevor would once more sacrifice himself when the time came, and *that*, Simon couldn't allow. "We're all adults here, Trev. I'm not a child who needs protection anymore," he said, whisper-quiet. "But even if I were, I want my big brother around."

Never the affectionate one, Trever nonetheless embraced him in a move so swift, it knocked the air from Simon's lungs. "I love you, Si. You are the best of us Blanes. Never forget it."

And with that, his brother was gone. Teleported off to goddess knew where to do whatever he thought might preserve Simon's life.

He stared in shock at the place where Trevor had been, not knowing how to follow. Blind fury brought on by fear boiled up inside, and Simon charged his father, shoving him back into the wall. "This is your fault!"

Ben didn't try to put up a fight. He could've, because they were built the same, with Ben being the more powerful of the two due to his abilities. But he didn't. The compassion in his eyes was off-putting.

"If anything happens to Trevor, I'll take it out of your ass, old man," Simon warned.

"If anything happens to Trevor, you won't need to. I'll do it for you," Damian said. "Now, enough talk. It's time Ben and I take a trip. Simon, you and Evelyn make use of O'Malley's inn tonight. It's Valentine's Day, after all."

"Wait, what?" Evelyn looked put out, and she checked her watch. "Oh. Right. Ireland time."

As much as it sucked to ignore a day dedicated to expressing his feelings for Evelyn, Simon didn't feel right taking a vacation from his problems. "We need to see this through," he said. "Clearing my name is too important right now, and we have to find Trev."

"I agree." She entwined her fingers with his in a show of solidarity. "Work first, play later."

He smiled down into her beloved face. "Thank you, Evelyn."

"I'll always have your back, Simon Says."

"And I'll always have yours."

"He'll be fine, Simon," Damian assured him. "Your brother has a destiny to fulfill above and beyond this situation. Take tonight for yourselves. Tomorrow will resolve itself. Trust me."

Simon wanted to, but he was wavering with the need to do something. *Anything* other than sit and wait. He'd been a supervisor at the Bureau, but he'd been active in takedowns. Sidelines were never his gig. The decision was made for him when his father stepped forward.

"I owe you and your brother this, son. My actions should never have resulted in the death of your mother or the end of your career."

Ben's gaze dropped to the floor, and his audible swallow shot straight to Simon's heart. The man before him was fit, still technically in his prime due to his magical genetics. But he also seemed beat down by life and jaded as fuck. In Simon's experience, those types of people didn't care if they lived or died.

Evelyn squeezed his hand, and Simon realized he'd waited too late for a casual reply. Propelled by some long-buried emotion, he tightly embraced his father. "Don't die, okay. Get in and get out, destroy that fucker Dutch, but don't die. My career means nothing next to your life," he said fiercely.

His father's arms came around him, and the two remained like that for a long moment. The boy, now grown, and the man who was a virtual shell of his former self. Tears burned Simon's eyes, and with one last squeeze, he cleared his throat and moved away.

"After I return, we'll restore your magic, Simon," Damian said. With a small smile and a wink, he added, "Enjoy your night."

A short bark of laughter escaped Simon and was exactly what he needed. But then, he figured the Aether, with his empath and telepathic abilities, already knew that. "Thank you, Damian."

After the two left, Simon faced Evelyn. "This goes against every fiber of my being."

"To let someone else handle our problem?" She nodded. "Yeah, mine, too. But oddly, I trust them to get it done, and frankly, your father *should* clean up his own mess."

"But I should be there with them."

"No, Simon. You don't have the magical firepower."

He winced, feeling less in her eyes.

"Don't do that," she scolded.

"What?"

"View yourself as unworthy. I imagine you've done it a lot in your lifetime. None of the past events were your fault. Not your mom, not your dad leaving, not your brother's recruitment into the Authority, and not your aunt's shooting." She cupped his jaw. "And certainly not Tiffany. Get rid of the baggage, Simon Says. It's way too heavy a burden to bear."

"Tiffany's death *is* my fault, Evelyn, and I can't dismiss it as easily as the other things." He heard the raggedness in his own voice, and it gave away what he'd been feeling since he learned he was a Death Dealer. "And despite what Isis said, or even what Damian may have predicted, I'm worried about you."

"Don't. I'm not. And Tiffany *wasn't* your fault," Evelyn stressed. "That's on the Authority for binding your power, and from what your father implied, not restoring it properly to you. Dealers can give life as well as take it. Had they not fucked up, Tiff would be here now."

"I don't think the guilt will ever go away," he confessed.

"I'll be there with you through the worst of it."

Her promise was the balm his wounded soul needed. He gave her a half-smile. "Well, you heard it from the Aether's mouth. We should make the best of our time here."

She grinned and snuggled into his embrace. "I was looking for any excuse to make love with you again."

"You never need one, babe. I'll always be waiting with open arms."

With a light, lingering kiss on his lips and a suggestive smile, Evelyn backed toward the door. "Let's go see about that room."

CHAPTER 31

"Here you go," Piper said as she unlocked and cracked the door to their suite. Her eyes sparkled with knowing as she looked between Evelyn and Simon. "Sheets are clean, and there's a little something special for you. Enjoy!" With a breezy wave of her hand, she left them in the hallway.

Evelyn was about to enter, but Simon stopped her with a hand on her arm.

"What's wrong?" she asked. A small part of her wondered if this forced romance was too much, too soon for him. Everyone—the Goddess and the Aether included—were shoving her at him and basically telling him they were going to be a couple. For Evelyn, their assumption wasn't a big deal. She'd loved Simon forever. But for a man still grieving his wife, who just discovered his father was very much alive and the career he worked so hard to build was precariously close to over, it might be overwhelming.

Simon's smile started slow and quickly spread to become an engaging grin.

Evelyn's worries fled.

"It's customary for a groom to carry his bride over the threshold of their honeymoon suite." His expression and voice were filled with love and a barely banked desire. "How about it, babe? Are you willing to be mine forever?"

"According to Alastair and Isis, we're already soul-bound."

"Yes, and no ceremony will ever be as beautiful as our night in the clearing," he said huskily. "For all intents and purposes, you're now my wife. But I need to hear it from you. I need to know if *you* want it as much as I do."

Joy filled her. She never dared hope he'd see her as anything other than a friend, but for him to say the words, to look at her as if she alone held the key to his eternal happiness, left her in little doubt of his true feelings.

"In that case, we should do this up right," she finally said. When he shifted to lift her, she stopped him with a hand on his chest. "You didn't get to see me in a wedding dress," she teased.

A wide grin split his face. "I'd rather see you out of your wedding dress."

"We can do both."

A frown drew his brows together, but the light dawned, and he chuckled. "Shall I turn my back while you whip one up?"

"Yes, please."

While his back was to her, Evelyn shot a look down the hallway to ensure they were alone. Then, she envisioned her perfect dress. Strapless, made of delicate lace with a push-up bodice held together in back by a wide, satin ribbon. The skirt was full and the threads so fine, they shimmered and sparkled even in the dim lighting. She swirled her hands around her head and lifted her arms, creating an upswept hairstyle pinned with a diamond clip, leaving a few wispy tendrils to soften the severity. Dangling earrings finished the look. Sparing a brief thought for shoes, she rejected the idea and settled on bare feet. Lastly, she glamoured her makeup to give her face added radiance.

When she was done, she called his name.

His awed expression was one she'd never forget. The reverence reflected in his tender gaze brought tears to her eyes, and she blinked rapidly to dispel the moisture, not wanting to destroy all her work.

"Stunning," he murmured softly. "Simply stunning. Thank you."

"Why are you thanking me?"

"Because you are a gift, Evelyn. Pure and simple. Your love, your willingness to spend your life with me despite the potential threat, it's the greatest treasure I'll ever receive and one I intend to cherish."

"I do love you, Simon. I think I always have."

He swung her up into his arms and brushed her nose in a butterfly kiss. "You've been my best friend for as long as I can remember, and now, we get to be so much more. An everlasting love."

Simon backed into the room with her securely cradled against his chest. After entering, he turned and kicked the door shut with his heel. It took her a second to register the delight on his face, and she turned her head to see what caused his smile. "Oh!"

Candles were strategically positioned around the space. A winding pathway of ruby-red rose petals led from a steaming bubble bath to a king-size bed. Next to the tub were two champagne flutes and a bottle sitting snuggled in a silver bucket filled with ice. A small tray of mini, personalized cakes rested on the foot of the bed. But the best part was the tree from Evelyn's apartment decorated with its sparkly pink decorations, illuminating the corner of their room.

Her heart filled to overflowing.

"Your cousin thought of everything but the condoms," he said dryly.

She took great pleasure in saying, "Witches don't need them."

"What?"

"We can't catch sexually transmitted diseases, and a condom won't stop the Goddess if she wants us to procreate."

He gave a happy shout of laughter. "That's the second-best news I've heard all day."

Her brows shot up. "Really? *That's* what makes you happy?"

"Babe, no man likes wearing a condom. It takes away part of our natural pleasure."

"I'll give you that one. And the best news—" she leaned in to nibble on his jaw "—clarify for me what that one was."

"You know damned well what it was, and I love you, too, Evelyn Thorne."

A knock sounded at their door.

Simon rubbed a hand over his face, then glanced at his watch.

Two-fifteen a.m.

He could've used a few more hours of sleep.

The knock sounded again, and Evelyn groaned as she burrowed her naked body closer to his.

Simon seriously thought about telling whoever was on the other side of that door to fuck all the way off, but he detangled himself from his clinging wife, kissed her forehead, and tucked her under the covers as she mumbled her complaint.

"Go back to sleep, babe," he said in a low voice. "I've got to see who's at the door."

"Tell them to fuck off," she said irritably.

Because her comment was so close to his thought, he laughed. "After all that wonderful lovemaking, you should be in a better mood," he teased as he drew on his jeans.

"You wore me out, and this was supposed to be our honeymoon. I'm selfish."

She sat up and pushed the hair from her eyes.

Simon caught his breath. Never had he seen such a beautiful sight.

Her hand brushed along the flat plane of his stomach, and his dick went on immediate alert.

"Evelyn," he said in a warning tone.

A mischievous smile curled her kiss-swollen lips. "Maybe they'll take the hint and go away, and you can come back to bed."

The third knock was louder and more insistent.

"Doesn't seem like they will." Simon captured Evelyn's wandering hands and brought them to his lips. "After. Promise."

"Fine," she said with a mock pout. "But don't expect any more sleep tonight."

"I'll consider myself warned." His grin lasted until he opened the door. The Aether was on the other side. "Dethridge. What is it? Is everything okay?"

"Everything is as I promised it would be. Your threat has been neutralized."

"Forever or for the moment?"

"Need you ask?" Damian replied in a dry as dirt tone. "Now, I'm tired and wish to get home. But there's the little matter of your abilities to resolve."

Simon glanced over his shoulder and noticed Evelyn was fully clothed and alert. He silently mourned her nude state.

Stepping back, he swung the door wide to grant access.

Damian's lips twitched as he got a look at the disheveled state of their room. "I see you made good use of your time." With a wave of his hand, he lifted Evelyn's forgotten wedding dress, and it floated to a nearby chair. When it settled over the back, it was free of wrinkles and pristine once again. "You should preserve that for future generations."

Simon blinked. Was the Aether saying he and Evelyn would have children? He shot her a questioning look, to which she shrugged, apparently unfazed either way.

"You mentioned restoring Simon's power," she said to Damian.

"Won't that take a ceremony? That's always been my understanding in the past."

"For anyone other than me, or for a larger restoration like the one needed for your family last year, yes. But this is a simple matter of an unbinding spell." He smiled at Simon, and there was pure deviltry in the look. "You'll want to lie down for this, or it'll knock you on your ass."

Suddenly wary of the potential power being handed back to him and the possible danger it posed, he asked, "This magic, can it be removed completely?"

Damian cocked his head slightly and narrowed his eyes as he studied Simon. "You're afraid."

"A little. You're about to give me a weapon I don't know how to wield, and you mentioned the restoration could be life threatening."

"I understand it can be intimidating and somewhat frightening. But it's your birthright, Simon. And I can't think of a finer man to own such a gift." He glanced between the two of them and finally clasped Simon's shoulder. "I'll tell you what. I'll give you tonight and tomorrow to think about it. When you've reached a decision, come see me. Whatever your preference, I'll make it happen."

"Thank you." Simon's gratitude was heartfelt, and he was sure Damian felt it. After they shook hands and the Aether kissed Evelyn's cheek, he left them alone.

Simon locked the door and stripped, determined to shelve the problem for another day. But Evelyn didn't let it go as easily as he'd have liked.

"Will you accept the Aether's gift?" she asked softly.

"Can't we do as Damian advised and think it over for a bit?" When she remained silent, waiting for his answer, Simon finally nodded. "I suppose I will, but not anytime soon. First, I want to know exactly what grief I'm setting myself up for."

Approaching her, he drew her shirt over her head. "And I believe I promised to make love as soon as our company left."

"Hmm, I might recall something of that nature," she said in a bored tone.

"How about you get you undressed and get your gorgeous ass in bed?" he suggested, knowing full well what her response would be.

She didn't disappoint.

With a wicked laugh, she shook her head. "Not until you say it properly."

"*Simon says* get undressed and get your gorgeous ass in bed."

AFTERWORD

Thank you for following the journey of my Thorne Witches series. If you're like me, you don't want to see them go away. Well, they're not! Going away, that is.

If you enjoyed this story, you're really going to love the next one, Captivating Magic! For more information check out my website: https://www.tmcromer.com/books/the-thorne-witches/captivating-magic.

Did you ever wonder about Liz's brothers? Well, the first of her three brothers will be getting his book. Look out for Laszlo Thorne's story, coming fall 2024 (or sooner).

Embittered warlock, Laszlo Thorne is saddled with the unique ability to bridge the gap between the living and the dead. It's a secret he guards closely to avoid novice paranormal hunters and charlatans alike. But when his sister's adorably quirky friend shows up and asks for an exorcism, he can't turn her away.

After a near-fatal accident, Ebba James is haunted by an apparition that blurs the lines of her reality. She's not convinced it isn't a figment of her overactive imagination. When she accidentally discovers the object of her embarrassing schoolgirl infatuation can communicate with the other side, she seeks Laszlo's help.

Amidst vengeful spirits and enigmatic mysteries, Ebba's decade-long crush fades and is replaced by a passion neither of them can deny. Unable to fight her captivating magic, Laszlo, once emotionally closed off, opens to the possibility of a second chance at happiness. Together, they navigate the shadowy depths of the supernatural, unveiling long-buried secrets that are better left alone.

Look for Captivating Magic starting summer 2024!

Also, if you haven't already subscribed to my **newsletter**, I encourage you to do so. It's the best way for you to stay current on upcoming stories. After I'm done with the O'Malleys, I'll be introducing the next generation of Thornes, and you won't want to miss it.

www.tmcromer.com/newsletter

Some of your favorite characters will be woven into my first Thorne Witches spinoff series, *The Unlucky Charms*, available now! Also, if you'd like to see more Damian Dethridge and his daughter, Beastie, be sure to preorder *The Aether*, book 1 in the *new* Thorne Witches spinoff series *Sentinels of Magic*, releasing October 2023.

Turn the page to read an excerpt of Piper Thorne and Cian O'Malley's love story, *Pints & Potions*.

When the mighty Thorne pricks the heart of the Frozen, the end will be set in motion...

Sick of the unwelcome attention that comes with being a member of an extremely powerful family, Piper Thorne longs to escape her magical burden and live a mortal's simple existence. On a whim, she adopts an alias and jets off to Ireland, where she stumbles into the path of the enticing rogue, Cian O'Malley. But she's ill prepared to deal with the onslaught of emotions his wicked grin stirs up when he oh-so-casually turns up the charm.

A hardened, down-on-his-luck warlock, Cian O'Malley is determined to change his family's plight and restore their stolen magic. In the midst of his half-baked plan to woo the bewitching Piper, he finds himself in a death match with an old enemy who's carrying a monumental grudge.

Before long, Cian discovers Piper might just hold the key to reversing a two-hundred-and-fifty-year-old curse. He only has to keep them both alive long enough to solve the riddle written in the O'Malleys' ancient grimoire and convince Piper to trust him with her heart.

Chapter One

"You need to hurry up, Piper. You're going to miss your flight. Although—"

"Don't say it," she snapped. She was currently lying belly down across the top of her overstuffed suitcase in an effort to make the edges meet. "I think I'm going to be over the weight limit."

"Take everything out but the sexy underwear," advised her cousin and best friend, Liz Thorne-Xuereb. "Or let me cast a spell to lighten the case."

"I don't have any sexy underwear." Piper willfully ignored the spell comment. She'd be damned if she would use magic for anything she didn't classify as an emergency. To do otherwise would be an abuse of power as far as she was concerned. Of course, her attitude wasn't popular among her family, who used magic with the speed of a ravenous chocoholic consuming bonbons.

Damn, she could really go for some lemon-buttercream chocolates to temper her traveling anxiety right about now.

"*At all?*" Liz screeched, pulling her back into the conversation. Her cousin was clearly appalled that a single woman wouldn't have the basics.

Heat crept up Piper's neck. "Well, I *do*, but not packed. It's *Ireland*, Liz. People dress in layers over there."

"Sure, but eventually they have to strip down—if you know what I mean. And thermal long johns aren't a turn on. What happens when you meet a hot Irishman and take him back to your hotel?"

"It's a B&B, and I won't be bringing any men back to my room. In case you failed to remember, I'm on a dating hiatus for a while. It's called *vacation* for a reason."

"Need I remind you that I found Rafe while on vacation?"

"Rafe found you, and he was in Paris on *business*."

Liz shrugged as she rummaged through Piper's dresser, looking for sexy articles of clothing. "You say tomato, I say tomahto."

"I'm pretty sure you stole that line from him. Regardless, I've sworn off men."

"Irish women are hot, too. Really, anyone with an Irish accent would do."

"You *know* what I mean. And while I'm open to just about anything, it's doubtful I'll switch sides midlife. Seriously, I just need a break from the dating game." Piper snatched the underwear out of

Liz's hands as she tried to add it to the suitcase. "Stop, or you really will make me late."

"Let's compromise. Take four matching sets."

"One."

"Three."

"Two and no thongs. I hate those things. They're little more than ass floss."

"Deal." Liz grinned triumphantly. "But if things get hot and heavy, I want a sex tape."

"Okay, *eww*, because you're my damned cousin. You're getting as bad as Mackenzie. Next thing you know, you'll be telling me you're into bondage." When Liz flushed the color of a ripe beet, Piper laughed. "I didn't know you had it in you!"

"It was only handcuffs," Liz retorted.

Piper arched her freshly waxed brows.

"All right, a blindfold, too. But that's all."

"Who was sporting the cuffs and blindfold? You or Rafe?"

"Rafe."

Tickled by the new carefree side of her cousin, Piper hugged Liz. "I'm so glad you found him. You deserved so much better than Franco."

"I still can't believe he stole my magic. Who *does* that?"

"Well, thankfully Rafe discovered his plan in time." She rounded up the last of her toiletries.

Liz cleared her throat, and Piper suspected it still stung her cousin's heart that her now-deceased boyfriend had tried to use her for nefarious purposes. "Enough with all the maudlin BS. Let's get this show on the road. Promise you'll FaceTime me from a local pub while you're sharing a drink with a local hottie."

Struggling against a laugh, Piper said, "I'm telling Rafe that he's not satisfying your urges if you're thinking about my sex life and hot Irishmen."

"Believe me, my woman's urges are completely taken care of—on every level." Rafe's sexy, slightly accented drawl came from the doorway and startled both of them.

Again, Liz flushed, and Piper was positive he spoke the truth. She sighed with the smallest hint of envy. Dark-brown hair, midnight-colored eyes, and six feet of sinewy body, Rafe was every woman's walking fantasy. However, he'd only had eyes for Liz from the day they reconnected a handful of years after their Paris meeting.

Feeling a bit warm herself, Piper returned to the bathroom to retrieve the last of her travel necessities. Once her carry-on was packed, she allowed Rafe to take both cases to the car. When he was out of earshot, she turned to Liz.

"You have to be the luckiest woman on the planet. Promise me I get him in your will should anything happen to you."

"Nope. I have a stipulation that he must mourn me forever. He's not allowed to find comfort with another woman."

"Now you're just being selfish."

They shared a laugh and headed out to join Rafe for the short ride to the airport.

After they arrived at the terminal, Rafe unloaded the cases from the truck and escorted Piper inside. "Remember, no taking candy from strangers. And any guy you're interested in has to provide you with a full name, date of birth, and some form of ID so I can scry and check him out. That way, we can avoid an incident like the last one."

Rafe was referring to Piper's shitty taste in men. Her crappy radar had failed to pick up on the fact her ex-boyfriend—a mortal one at that—was married with a baby on the way.

"Got it," Piper responded with a grin and a hug. "Thanks, Rafe."

"Be safe and call us when you get settled. Liz and I want to know when you arrive, okay? Although, why you don't teleport is beyond me." He glanced around and lowered his voice. "Don't use the name Thorne. Lie if you have to. It isn't safe to bandy about that name when you are on your own, even in this day and age."

"I'll be plain old Piper Kelly. I plan to vacation like a normal person. And I promise to let you both know when I arrive."

Rafe shook his head. "This crazy need of yours to be 'normal' baffles me. We're magical beings. You should embrace your heritage."

It was an old argument between her and her family. It seemed

Rafe had taken their side. No one would ever understand. In a family full of the most powerful witches on the planet, Piper got lost. Not bothering to answer, she kissed his cheek and hugged Liz.

Two and a half hours later, Piper was boarded and on her way to Ireland for her much-needed dream vacation. Two weeks in the Emerald Isle with nothing to do but enjoy the countryside, eat fish and chips, and listen to Irish folk bands play in local pubs. No corporate crap, no IT problems popping up from employees who could barely log into their email accounts. Most importantly, no running into her ex-boyfriend at work or his pregnant wife at their hometown supermarket.

Piper would take the time to lick her wounds and formulate a new plan for a family of her own. Perhaps it was time to rule out a lifelong mate and go with artificial insemination. That way, she would be able to pick a sperm donor based on genetics and brains instead of waiting for Mr. Wrong to come along for what seemed like the millionth time. Goddess willing, by this time next year, she planned to be a mom. It didn't get more normal than that, right?

The idea had a soft smile forming on her lips. The thought of holding her own newborn close and rocking him or her to sleep made Piper's heart ping. All she'd ever wanted was a family to love. At thirty-three, her biological clock wasn't only ticking; it was setting off alarms on an hourly basis.

But first, she'd take one last vacation before her world would be forever altered by a baby. Afterwards, her life wouldn't be her own, and she intended to live it up on this holiday while she still could.

Cian O'Malley didn't miss much. From early on, he'd trained himself to gauge the energy of the pub's patrons and work the room. From his position on stage, he noted the stranger among the standard Friday-night crowd. He caught sight of the black-haired beauty the moment she stepped into his pub. Her light honey eyes were bright with excitement, and he immediately recognized that she wasn't from around these parts. Mainly because he knew almost everyone who was. He also recognized the magical glow around her. With such a bright, blinding aura, she had to be a witch—a powerful one at that. If he was mistaken, he'd eat his microphone.

As he picked out a lively tune and sang about a love gone wrong in a way only the Irish could, he tracked her with his eyes. Before this night was out, he intended to not only know her name but also steal a kiss from those glossy, beguiling lips of hers.

His sister Bridget served the stranger a Guinness, and he nearly laughed at the face the woman made upon taking her first sip. A pint of plain wasn't for the faint of heart. But he had to give her credit for trying the dark brew.

The noise of the room abruptly faded away, and her American accent drifted to where he sat. As he transitioned from one song to the next, he watched his new obsession laugh and flirt with some of the other male patrons. Aye, he'd be settling up with those plonkers later for making time with the woman Cian had mentally claimed as his own.

Soon enough, his set was finished, and he made his way through the swell of customers and friends slapping him on the back. When he was less than five feet from her, the dark-haired siren turned her merry eyes upon him. It was as if lightning struck at that moment, and Cian found it impossible to catch his breath. His only consolation was her own dumbstruck expression. She felt the connection as well.

Good to know he wasn't the only fool for love.

"Well, hello, darlin'. I see you've been enjoyin' yerself in me pub." He laid the accent on thick because American women turned to mush after hearing his honeyed Irish tongue.

With sparkling eyes, she asked, "Your pub? So you're *the* O'Malley in Lucky O'Malley's Pub?"

"One of them. Cian O'Malley at your service, darlin'. And whom do I have the pleasure of speakin' with in turn?"

"Piper Kelly."

"Ah, to be sure, you must be a good Irish *cailín* with a name like Kelly."

Her laughter was as golden as her aura. The sound reached in and grabbed him by the nads, making him lose all sense of up or down.

"Does this…" She made a swirling gesture with her hand around his mouth. "…actually work to help you pick up women?"

He placed his palm flat over his heart. "You wound me, darlin'. You surely do."

"Uh-huh." She sounded doubtful, but his soon-to-be woman had a twinkle in her eye, which clearly indicated she liked his suffering.

"Put a man out of his misery and run away with me, why don't ya?"

"I'm sure your wife wouldn't appreciate that." She gestured with her thumb over her shoulder to Bridget, who stood behind the bar, giving him the evil eye.

"Bridget isn't my wife, love. She's my sister. And the look she's gracing us with is because she's vexed I'm passing time with you and not servin' up these louts hangin' about me bar."

"Pull on your wellies, lads," Bridget called out. "It's about to get deep in here because Cian intends to rabbit on in hopes of catching a ride!"

"Ride?" Piper questioned just before taking a sip of her pint.

He mentally debated the merits of honesty when the ginger-haired Seamus, sitting on the stool beside her, spoke up and beat him to the punch. "Shag. Cian's hopin' to shag ye."

Guinness sprayed the air as Piper choked on her drink. Seamus earned a dark glare from Cian as he snatched up a dry bar towel to mop the beer from his face.

"Dry up this mess and don't be annoying me, Seamus, or you'll be finding yourself out on your arse," Cian growled and threw down the damp towel.

"Jaysus, Cian! Don't be hasty," Seamus exclaimed, rushing to comply. "It was Bridget who said it."

"And it was *you* who were repeating it, you feckin' eejit."

"Is this always the way you woo women?" Piper asked.

Her grin was as bright as the morning sun on a clear summer day, and Cian found himself soaking up its warmth.

"If we're being honest, no. I'm much more smooth and charming."

"Good to know you weren't banking on your looks alone."

Although they were in a crowded place, Cian only had eyes for this lone woman. The tilt of her head and the half smile still lingering on her lips fascinated him. She was, without a doubt, flirting in return. Ah, the sight of her sped up his heart. It truly did.

"Love, I have a bet with a few of me mates." He laid it on thick, but he was savvy enough to recognize she was enjoying their exchange. "It's a well-known fact that me boyos look up to me in these parts."

"Uh-huh." She sounded cynical but amused. "So what's this bet?"

"Well, it's more of a tradition, really," he lied. "I'm forced to kiss all the new colleens who stroll into me pub."

"*Forced* to?"

"Aye, and if I can win a kiss from the fairest of women—that be you—I'd be a living legend in these parts."

"Still not seeing where the bet part of this comes in."

"I bet me boyos that you'd take mercy on me and bestow the kiss to end all kisses."

"Interesting. When exactly did you make this bet? Because since I've been here, you've been on stage or here beside me."

Cian could see his sister smirk from the corner of his eye. The pub had grown quiet to watch the interplay between Piper and him.

"She has you there, Cian!" someone hollered.

"It's implied," Cian informed her without missing a beat, ignoring his heckler.

Her left brow practically shot to her hairline, and she bit one corner of the plump lip he was dying to sample.

"One taste, darlin'. That's all I'm hoping for. Then I can die a happy man," he said softly.

"Who am I to stand in the way of tradition?"

He wasn't sure he heard her correctly, but he didn't give her a chance to change her mind. Swooping in, hands cupping her exquisite face, he claimed his prize. When their lips connected, warning bells sounded in his brain. This long-legged dream of a woman was dangerous to his well-being.

Her arms went around his neck, and her fingers wound their way through his hair. Her light caress of his scalp sent desire ricocheting through his entire body. He tightened his hold on her, and had his eyes been open, he'd have closed them in ecstasy. Hoots and catcalls sounded around them, but Cian was damned if he could sever their connection.

Until a cold blast of water from his right side dampened his ardor.

"Bridget, you she-devil!" he swore.

"Stop mauling the customers and get back to strumming. We have a pub to entertain."

"Oh, you can be sure we were entertained, *mo ghrá!*" A male voice called out from a table in the far back reaches of the pub.

"I'm not your love, Ruairí O'Connor. And you'd best be remembering your manners in my pub."

"I'd be your everything if you'd let me, Bridg," Ruairí returned.

"Pfft." She rolled her eyes. "Right. Me and every other woman within a hundred-kilometer radius." Bridget winked in Piper's direction. "Don't believe any of these wankers, girl. They delight in pulling your leg. My brother Cian is the worst of the lot. You're the fifth woman he's hit on this week."

Piper turned disappointed eyes on him but didn't look surprised.

Cian felt a tightening in his chest and scowled his sister from where he stood behind Piper. "Now, don't be spreading tales, Bridget. You'll have my darlin' Piper believing the worst of us." He swept aside the hair from Piper's neck and leaned in to whisper. "Ignore her. She's out to kick a man in the bollocks on her best day. Will you stick around for my next set? I'll dedicate a song to you."

"It's been a long day. Maybe next time," she demurred, apology heavy in her voice.

Although it sounded as if she'd like nothing better than to hang out for another beer and to flirt with him, she also looked like she was on her last leg.

"Are you stayin' local?"

She nodded. "For a few days."

"Good. I'll walk you back to your hotel."

"No need, I'm only right next door at the B&B."

"Humor me."

The steely tone caused her frown and most likely had her wondering where his charming Irish accent had gone. She was clever enough to realize he laid it on a little thicker for the tourists, and Cian surmised it was why she didn't say anything.

"You can trust him to walk you to your room, Piper," Bridget assured her as she built another Guinness at the tap. "He knows if he disappears on me, there'll be the devil to pay." Addressing Cian, Bridget warned, "Five minutes. Any longer, and I'll come for you myself."

Seamus snorted and said, "Five minutes? More than three be one too many for Cian."

Cian shoved him off the barstool.

Seamus had the reflexes of a cat, and the man didn't spill a drop of his beer. "What? I was meaning to get into the gal's—"

Cian clamped a hand over Seamus's mouth. "I ken what you were meaning. You'd do well to shut your pie hole, Seamus McCleary." He released his drunk friend with a second none-too-gentle shove. "He's cut off."

"Ye got a mean streak as wide as—"

"Not another word, Seamus," Cian growled.

"You've wasted two of your five minutes, brother."

"Come on, love. I don't want you to be a witness to murder."

Cian placed his hand on Piper's lower back and guided her toward the door. A current of sorts passed between them, shocking him, and he sent her a sharp glance to see if she'd experienced the same.

She appeared unfazed.

A simple touch had never set him off before. Dry-mouthed, he held his own council and silently walked with her toward the building next door.

"You handled that well," she said as he strolled beside her.

Surprised, he stopped and stared. His laughter, when it started, was deep and boomed out across the night. The sound carried and seemed to echo forever. He reached for her hand and placed a lingering kiss on her fingertips. "Come, let's get you home."

ALSO BY T.M. CROMER

Get your printable list on my website:

https://www.tmcromer.com/printable-booklist

Books in The Thorne Witches Series:

SUMMER MAGIC

AUTUMN MAGIC

WINTER MAGIC

SPRING MAGIC

REKINDLED MAGIC

LONG LOST MAGIC

FOREVER MAGIC

ESSENTIAL MAGIC

MOONLIT MAGIC

ENCHANTED MAGIC

CELESTIAL MAGIC

EVERLASTING MAGIC

CAPTIVATING MAGIC

Books in The Thorne Witches: Happily Ever Afters Series:

ENDURING MAGIC

BOUNDLESS MAGIC

Books in The Unlucky Charms Series:

PINTS & POTIONS

WHISKEY & WITCHES

BEER & BROOMSTICKS

www.ingramcontent.com/pod-product-compliance
Lightning Source LLC
Chambersburg PA
CBHW071937190726
48293CB00004B/1269